MY HERO

5 t h   U . A .

ACADEMIA

Report

MY HERO ACADEMIA

SCHOOL BRIEFS

5

ORIGINAL STORY BY
KOHEI HORIKOSHI

WRITTEN BY
ANRI YOSHI

Underground Dungeon

U.A. HIGH SCHOOL

Hero Course: Class 1-A

Izuku Midoriya

Birthday: July 15
Quirk: One For All

Katsuki Bakugo

Birthday: April 20
Quirk: Explosion

Shoto Todoroki

Birthday: January 11
Quirk:
Half-Cold Half-Hot

Tenya Ida

Birthday: August 22
Quirk: Engine

Fumikage Tokoyami

Birthday: October 30
Quirk: Dark Shadow

Minoru Mineta

Birthday: October 8
Quirk: Pop Off

Ochaco Uraraka

Birthday:
December 27
Quirk: Zero Gravity

Momo Yaoyorozu

Birthday:
September 23
Quirk: Creation

Tsuyu Asui

Birthday: February 12
Quirk: Frog

Yuga Aoyama

Birthday: May 30
Quirk: Navel Laser

Mina Ashido

Birthday: July 30
Quirk: Acid

Mashirao Ojiro

Birthday: May 28
Quirk: Tail

Denki Kaminari

Birthday: June 29
Quirk: Electrification

Eijiro Kirishima

Birthday: October 16
Quirk: Hardening

Koji Koda

Birthday: February 1
Quirk: Anivoice

Rikido Sato

Birthday: June 19
Quirk: Sugar Rush

Mezo Shoji

Birthday: February 15
Quirk: Dupli-Arms

Kyoka Jiro

Birthday: August 1
Quirk: Earphone Jack

Hanta Sero

Birthday: July 28
Quirk: Tape

Toru Hagakure

Birthday: June 16
Quirk: Invisibility

Hero Course: Class 1-B

Itsuka Kendo

Birthday:
September 9
Quirk: Big Fist

Neito Monoma

Birthday: May 13
Quirk: Copy

Tetsutetsu Tetsutetsu

Birthday: October 16
Quirk: Steel

Ibara Shiozaki

Birthday:
September 8
Quirk: Vines

Nirengeki Shoda

Birthday: February 2
Quirk: Twin Impact

Setsuna Tokage

Birthday: October 13
Quirk:
Lizard Tail Splitter

Pony Tsunotori

Birthday: April 21
Quirk: Horn Cannon

Kinoko Komori

Birthday: December 2
Quirk: Mushroom

Hero Course: Faculty

Shota Aizawa

Birthday: November 8
Quirk: Erasure

Midnight

Birthday: March 9
Quirk: Somnambulist

Present Mic

Birthday: July 7
Quirk: Voice

Thirteen

Birthday: February 3
Quirk: Black Hole

MY HERO ACADEMIA

SCHOOL BRIEFS

5

CONTENTS

Underground Dungeon

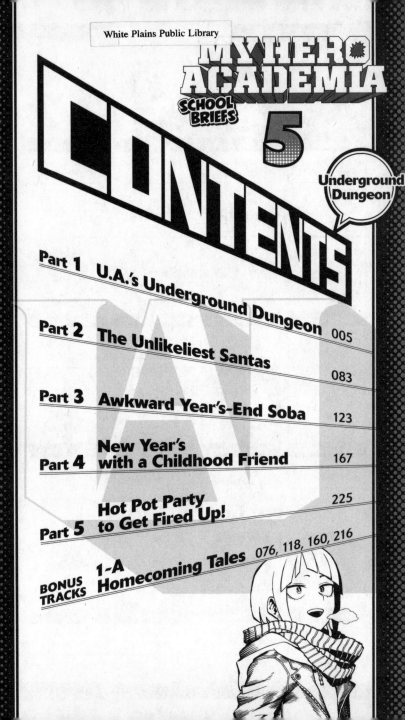

Part 1
U.A.'s Underground Dungeon

The cold, dry air at the end of the calendar year isn't ideal for an active lifestyle, and while wild animals instinctively take it easy during this season, people are somehow busier than ever. For instance, take that hallmark of the year's end in Japan—the big winter cleaning.

U.A.'s School Festival had ended without incident (relatively speaking), and Endeavor had formally taken up the mantle of number one hero. At first, he didn't receive the warm public opinion once enjoyed by his predecessor and the Symbol of Peace, All Might, but following the number two hero, Hawks, down to Hakata was the first step to changing that. The two found themselves locked in a battle to the death against a High-End Nomu, and ever since, the public's general unease over the absence of the Symbol of Peace had been steadily replaced with support for Endeavor. The run-in with the High-End had been no mere coincidence, however. Behind the scenes, Hawks was making contact with the League of Villains (at the request of the Heroes Public Safety Commission), and engineering this battle had been a loyalty test of sorts.

Right around when classes 1-A and 1-B were facing off in their joint battle training, the Metahuman Liberation Army had come under the control of the League of Villains, giving rise to a new organization called the Paranormal Liberation Front. The Safety Commission had become aware of Tomura Shigaraki's newfound resources and his scheme to destroy society and the status quo, but out of the large number of heroes and hero fledglings with provisional licenses who would soon launch an all-out attack on the P.L.F., only a small fraction had any idea about what was to come.

In fact, nobody at U.A. High knew about these dark machinations at the moment, which was just as well, since the students were already occupied enough with the big

winter cleaning. Within the dorm buildings, they had their own rooms—personal spaces marked by unique aesthetic choices that represented their personalities. Regularly cleaning these rooms was up to the individual, of course, and though tidiness was generally linked to soundness of body and mind, clearly not every student lived by that creed. Some cleaned their rooms every day, some every two or three days, some once a week, some once a month—while still other stubborn souls had never once cleaned their rooms since moving into the dorms. Those who made exceptional efforts to keep their spaces clean had already finished the winter cleaning, including class 1-A's president, Tenya Ida.

"There we go. All the books I've finished reading," he said, as he tied a stack of books with string and placed the bundle in a cardboard box.

A satisfied "job well done" smile rose on his face. Though Ida was never one to neglect day-to-day tidying, even he was prone to procrastinating when it came to cleaning his desk, his bookshelves, the space behind his bed, and the gutter out on the veranda, so he felt unusually refreshed as he surveyed his now impeccably clean room.

All that remained was to mail the box of books to his family. Ida's "to read" pile had shrunk considerably, so he would have to ask his mother to ship over another bundle or two of new reading material. With the box in his arms, he left the room, but a cry from next door stopped him in his tracks.

"Ugh! I've done it now..." came the voice of his neighbor Mashirao Ojiro.

"Whatever is the matter?" asked Ida, peeking through the open door. Ojiro had clearly been wiping down the floor with a rag, but the tip of his tail was soaking wet. Ida's look changed from alarm to concern.

"My tail took a dip in the bucket of dirty water," said Ojiro.

"That's a shame," said Ida. "Let me fetch you a towel."

"Ah, no need. I'll clean myself off in the bathroom since I've gotta rinse the rags anyway."

After wringing out his tail tip like a washcloth, Ojiro got back to cleaning, prompting a soft smile from Ida. Box still in hand, he kept walking down the hallway on his mission toward the first floor, but he was stopped once again, this time by some peppy music and a loud "Oooh..." coming from Denki Kaminari's room.

This door was also ajar, and Ida spotted his floor mate reading a magazine.

"I suppose your cleaning is coming along swimmingly, Kaminari?"

"Sure is! But y'see, I was sorting my mags, and I stumbled across this one," replied Kaminari.

He turned the magazine around, showing Ida a page with an interview of the Laundry Hero: Wash and the Equipped Hero: Yoroi Musha. Though Wash's answers were all some form of "Washashasha," Yoroi Musha had been more than willing and able to share his thoughts and feelings with the interviewer.

"I skimmed through this the first time—lotsa words, y'know?—but now that I'm reading it for real, there are some great insights here," said Kaminari. "Wanna check it out?"

Ida's curiosity was piqued, but he had a greater concern at the moment.

"That's all well and good, Kaminari, but aren't you in the middle of cleaning?"

"Well, sure. But until I finish reading this, how'm I s'posed to know if it goes in the trash or the 'keep' pile?"

"You'll never finish the task unless you learn to sort more quickly! In fact... Oh dear—look how many magazines you have left. And, hrm? Is that dust I spy in the corner? Even your skateboard is coated in it! Don't tell me...you haven't even begun to tackle the veranda?"

"Uhh, the veranda's not exactly on my to-do list. Who cares?"

"If enough dry leaves have been deposited in your gutter by the wind, then the gutter will fail to serve its purpose during the next rainstorm!" explained Ida.

"Dang, really? But how's a guy even s'posed to clean out the gutter, of all things?"

First, remove the debris, thought Ida, but before he could begin his next lecture, he glanced around the room again.

There's little sense in jumping ahead to the veranda when the room itself is still a mess, right? In which case, why don't I just...

Ida was fully prepared to dive in and offer to help Kaminari clean, but he stopped himself at the last second.

Proper cleaning is a component of self-discipline! My helping Kaminari would be decidedly against his own interests!

Rather than rob a friend of a chance for self-improvement, Ida turned to Kaminari and said, "I have tools for cleaning the veranda in my room. They are yours to use, if you'd like."

"Oh, y'mean it? Thanks."

Ida returned Kaminari's carefree thank-you with a smile and left the room.

If he hasn't finished by the end of the day, I can help tomorrow.

The class president was always reluctant to abandon a constituent in need.

As Ida rode in the elevator from the third to the first floor, Izuku Midoriya was in his second-floor dorm room, lovingly wiping down the All Might figures that adorned the various surfaces there. The boy didn't just have reverence for All Might as a mentee—he was also a die-hard fan. He wanted to know every last detail about the man. He cherished All Might merchandise, and he would gladly dive into a swimming pool full of the merch, if possible, though certainly not at the expense of scratching any of it. Yes, he was a fanboy beyond hope, and it had become something of a yearly tradition for Midoriya to dust and wipe his All Might products during the big winter cleaning. That turned the time spent cleaning into a labor of love that brought him nothing short of bliss. Those action figures watched over him day in and day out, and he'd lost count of how many times the mere sight of them had brought him peace and encouraged him to try just a little harder.

Thank you for all you do, thought Midoriya with a small smile. Naturally, his appreciation was directed not only at the pieces of plastic but also at the man himself.

"Midoriya."

Midoriya spun around at the sound of his name to find Shoto Todoroki peering through the open door.

"What's up, Todoroki?"

"I found this mechanical pencil. Is it yours?"

"Oh, sure is," said Midoriya. "I must've dropped it when you were helping me out with English the other day? Anyway, thanks for bringing it back. I take it you're all done cleaning?"

"Yeah," came Todoroki's nonelaborative answer. He stood still for a moment, his eyes scanning Midoriya's room.

"You really do have a lot. All Might stuff, I mean," he said.

Midoriya somehow managed to detect a note of admiration in Todoroki's voice, so he decided to take the comment as a compliment.

"I guess so," he said, scratching the back of his head as he blushed.

"Maybe I could use one of these things for my room."

Todoroki's offhand comment sparked a glint in Midoriya's eyes.

"Oh? For your own room?! I have just the thing!" said the fanboy, zipping straight to his closet like an arrow in flight before extracting a figure still in its box. One trait of fanboys is their need to propagate more of their kind. They delight at any opportunity to do so. It's a remarkably pure desire that seems to spring from their love of spreading the joys of fandom.

"This one came out early in the Golden Age!" began Midoriya, practically snorting with excitement. "Limited edition, which means they didn't make a lot of them!

Anyway, check it out! The eyebrows—at that angle, spaced just like that—create an expression brimming with confidence! And that All Might smile! You can't help but grin at it yourself! They even used a newly developed type of paint to replicate that particular gleam on his teeth! See how it sparkles when I shift it around under the light?! And don't get me started on the detailed muscle lines! One look tells you that he's packing enough power to send villains flying with a single punch! Not to mention the hair! Or the cape, which flutters so naturally! They even paid attention to the poses of his fingers! And didja notice how they got the costume color just right? To the point that, honestly, I wouldn't be shocked if this little guy popped right out of the box to fight crime! It's pretty darn clear how much love was put into crafting this, right? I wish I could run off right now and find those artists to thank them for a job well done! Every fan worth their weight pretty much drools over this figure! Well, what do you say?!"

With the monologue over, Midoriya finally took a much-needed breath as Todoroki thought for a moment.

"Why don't you have this one out on display?" asked Todoroki.

"I'd love to!" said Midoriya. "But also not, if you catch my drift? Something this rare has to be treasured, and it just feels more right to admire it in secret."

"Then in that case—" began Todoroki, and instantly Midoriya realized that his friend was about to turn down the offer of the apparently nondisplayable figure.

"Ah, don't get me wrong! I'm offering...because I have two of them!"

Midoriya spun around and plucked an identical box from the closet with a "ta-da" flourish.

"You see, my mom didn't realize that I'd already bought it for myself, so she went and stood in line for hours to get me the perfect birthday present. No sense in displaying both of them, so you're welcome to take one off my hands."

There was an element of bashfulness in the offering, and Todoroki stared at the figure, paused, and shook his head.

"But what if I dropped it and broke it? No, just forget it."

"Oh. Okay..." said a dejected Midoriya.

"But can I drop by to look at it sometime?"

"Yeah, sure! Of course!"

Midoriya's full-throttle smile managed to soften Todoroki's expression a little, but before either could say another word, a new voice sang out from the doorway.

"Yoo-hoo! If you intend to gaze upon treasures, I shall lend you my sparkle light. ☆"

Midoriya's next-door neighbor, Yuga Aoyama, had apparently overheard the conversation and now directed a beam from some sort of handheld spotlight directly at the All Might figure. At the sight of the illuminated figure, Midoriya's dinner-plate-sized eyes grew to serving platters.

"Bright Might!" he said. "That's amazing, Aoyama!"

"Oh, neat," said Todoroki, genuinely impressed despite his unchanging expression.

"Hey, Aoyama," came a new voice from the hallway. It was filled with unbridled desire. "Why not shine your light on *my* rare treasure…?"

Minoru Mineta, the embodiment of lust, swaggered up and tried to shove a page of a lewd magazine into the beam's path. When Midoriya noticed the contents, he blushed fiercely, shielded his own eyes, and said, "Y-you can't have that sort of magazine, Mineta!"

"Oh, stuff it," said Mineta. "Maybe the right sorta light would expose everything, if you know what I mean! Just, like, baring it all... Which would be great, but, hmm... Maybe having some stuff hidden fires up the imagination, y'know? Like how even after the music stops playing, there's still a recording of it? There's just something about this paper, this analog media, these photos—that capture the true sexiness of babes' bodies!"

With a voracious look on his face, Mineta kept pushing his magazine closer to the light source, illuminating it from behind. Aoayama gasped and recoiled in disgust at his classmate's zeal, but Mineta didn't care. His eyes were practically pressed against the paper when the light's heat ignited the magazine.

"Whoa! M-my eyes! My eyes!"

Mineta dropped to the floor, writhing around, and Todoroki wasted no time in blasting the burning magazine with a shot of ice.

"You okay?" asked Todoroki.

"Not burned, I hope?!" cried Midoriya.

As his concerned classmates gathered around, Mineta shot back up, shocked but not injured by the fire.

"Didn't see that coming," he said, sounding relieved, but then he spotted what used to be his magazine—now a burned and frozen clump of paper—and exploded.

"Argh! My rare treasure!"

UA

"Did you just hear a scream?" asked Ida.

He had made it to the first floor and was now speaking to Koji Koda just in front of the elevator.

"Nuh-uh," said Koda, shaking his head. He held a black garbage bag filled with the sand that served as litter for his pet rabbit, Yuwai. Being a responsible pet owner meant that Koda was another student who dutifully cleaned his room daily.

"Perhaps not, then..." said Ida, who was now contemplating checking up on his classmates' cleaning progress, as any good class president would. That's when he spotted Eijiro Kirishima dragging something toward the entryway.

"And what might that be, Kirishima?" asked Ida.

"Just hauling my busted punching bag off to the garbage," answered Kirishima with a smile, gasping for breath. The punching bag weighed at least one hundred kilograms, not including the stand, which was dented and bent past the point of usefulness.

"How on earth did your equipment end up that way?" asked Ida.

"Got a little too fired up during training, I guess?" said a glum Kirishima, scratching his head.

Ida's and Koda's eyes popped. It would take quite a bit of "fire" to warp the punching bag's sturdy stand, but Ida was impressed by what this implied about Kirishima's training regimen.

"I suppose I shouldn't be surprised that you train in your own room!" he said.

"These muscles don't lie, dude! And there's nothing more trustworthy than good ol' fashioned hard work!" said Kirishima.

"What a shame, though," said Ida. "No more training for you, now that your equipment is broken, right?"

"Not to worry! You can buy anything online, so I'll have another one before you know it," said Kirishima cheerily as he continued dragging the punching bag toward the front door. Seeing Kirishima's braced legs shuffle awkwardly, Ida set his box down, ran over, and grabbed one end of the heavy load.

"Allow me to assist."

"Eh? You mean it? Weren't you in the middle of something or whatever?"

"My task can wait, and this is far more efficient."

"I can grab the other side," said Koda. He slung the bag of rabbit litter over his shoulder and gripped part of the punching bag stand.

"Dang, you really don't gotta! But thanks?" said Kirishima, as if he could hardly believe his good fortune.

"No reason not to help each other out," said Koda as the three boys started moving toward the garbage area.

"How is your cleaning effort coming along, Kirishima?" asked Ida.

"I wish I could say 'just dandy,' but I ain't so great about sweating the small stuff. Not like Bakugo, who was up there scrubbing every little nook and cranny."

"Ah, despite what one might assume, Bakugo does have an eye for detail," said Ida. "When he and Midoriya were under house arrest, he was sure to clean every corner of our home away from home."

They walked beneath the leaden winter air, talking about everything and nothing. The boys remarked on their white, faintly visible breath, they said hi to a cat who had decided to settle down on the U.A. grounds, and they chatted about effective training regimens, their academic studies, distinguishing the several moods of Aizawa Sensei, and even the dinner menu.

"Hmm?" said Koda, prompting the other two to notice Fumikage Tokoyami up ahead. He was carrying a large paper bag and immediately realized where his classmates must be going with the busted training equipment.

"The usual garbage spot is full," said Tokoyami. He had his own trash to dispose of but had been forced to seek out the provisional dumping area, set up to accommodate any overflow during the big winter cleaning.

"I believe this is our garbage's new destination," said Tokoyami, showing a map on his phone to the other three. It looked to be at the edge of the woods, not far from the dorms. Apparently the info had just been sent to all students, but Ida, Koda, and Kirishima hadn't brought their phones, since they'd assumed the chore wouldn't take them long.

"We're lucky we ran into you," said Ida with a decisive nod.

The trio was now a quartet, and they proceeded toward the provisional dump, now with Tokoyami's "Dark Shadow" also supporting part of the punching bag. The chitchat continued until they came across one of their teachers, Power Loader, sitting on a bench. He was alone, drinking a canned coffee, with an empty instant ramen container at his side. The boys said hello, prompting Power Loader to wave awkwardly before scampering back to the staff lodgings. The teachers were doing their own cleaning today as well.

"Why dine outside when it's so chilly?" wondered Ida aloud with a tilt of his head.

"Change of pace, maybe? Like, to wake himself up?" suggested Kirishima. Ida seemed convinced enough, and Tokoyami changed the subject.

"Have you three felt the small earthquakes at night recently?"

Koda gasped and nodded, but Ida and Kirishima simply turned to each other and shrugged.

"I have not," said Ida. "Perhaps because I make a point of going to sleep early each night?"

"Same here. After training, it's a quick bath, then snoozeville," said Kirishima.

Tokoyami looked puzzled and said, "I see... How odd. I've been checking my phone for any reports of earthquakes, but I haven't seen any."

"Maybe just your imagination, dude?" suggested Kirishima.

"That was my thought at first, but my imagination can't be responsible for nearly twenty instances..." said Tokoyami, sounding gravely serious about the matter.

Ida turned to Koda for his take, which the latter offered timidly.

"Jiro said that she hears a strange noise during each little earthquake. Like something's breaking somewhere. Or maybe scraping, or grinding..."

Kyoka Jiro's "Earphone Jack" Quirk allowed her to pick up even the faintest sounds, and the boys knew that testimony from someone so skilled at reconnaissance shouldn't be taken lightly.

"What on earth could it be...?" wondered Ida.

Assuming the phenomenon were really happening, was it something natural or not? This question nagged at Ida and made his brow furrow, but his thoughts were interrupted by a jangling and rattling that approached from behind.

"Garbage run?" asked Mezo Shoji, who held a number of cardboard boxes with arms produced by his "Dupli-Arms" Quirk. It was an odd sight since everyone knew that Shoji was an avowed minimalist who didn't own enough stuff to fill that many boxes. He noticed the boys' stares and answered before they could ask, explaining that he had finished cleaning his own room as well as the communal bath and kitchen before offering to take out the girls' trash for them, as they hadn't finished their cleaning yet.

The five began walking again, and the gang asked their newest member about the mini earthquakes and strange noises.

"I was wondering about that too," said Shoji. "The noises are too faint to pinpoint, though."

Since Shoji's Quirk let him produce extra eyes and ears at the ends of his tentacles, he was another classmate skilled at scouting, so the fact that both he and Jiro were still in the dark about this phenomenon told them they would ignore it at their own peril.

"I can't claim to know what's going on, but we ought to inform Aizawa Sensei posthaste, once we're finished out here," said Ida.

The group finally reached the backup trash spot near the woods and placed the punching bag near the edge of the small pile that was steadily forming. Shoji deftly set down the cardboard boxes, and instantly Tokoyami's gaze was drawn to a bat-shaped decoration in one of them.

"Could that be...Batboy?!" asked Tokoyami, barely able to contain his excitement. He put down his paper bag and reached for the object.

"Ooh, that brings me back," said Kirishima with a sparkle in his eye.

"What is 'Batboy,' dare I ask?" said a confused Ida.

"A real popular American movie from way back when," said Kirishima. "Batboy! The kid superhero who controls bats! Kinda cool how he was more of a dark hero, y'know. You've never seen that flick?"

"Apologies. I'm woefully ignorant when it comes to most entertainment," said Ida.

"So lemme guess, Tokoyami—you're a Batboy fan?" asked Kirishima.

"Indeed... The young loner who commands jet-black bats to carry out justice. A character I admire very much."

Passion filled Tokoyami's voice, as if this talk had revived within him emotions from years past. But then his paper bag fell over and its contents spilled out, including ripped black clothing, a tapestry with a geometric pattern, and a crystal ball about ten centimeters wide. Though the ground was relatively flat, the slight slope began to carry away the rolling ball.

"Ah, my Dark Night Crystal!" cried Tokoyami, but it had already rolled into the nearby woods. As he rushed off in pursuit, Ida tilted his head and raised a question.

"That looked to me like an ordinary transparent crystal ball, so what exactly was 'dark' or 'night'-like about it?"

Kirishima shook his head as if to say, "Don't ask, man."

"It's cuz, y'know..."

"I know what, exactly?" said Ida.

"There's a time in a kid's life when he's just gotta give names like that to stuff..." explained Kirishima. Ida still wasn't entirely sure what that meant, but he could accept that everyone went through phases. It just

so happened that during the height of Tokoyami's middle schooler syndrome, the boy had named the crystal ball after the hero he idolized—Dark Crystal.

A murder of cawing crows flew overhead. Tokoyami still hadn't returned.

"You think he's okay?" asked Koda, glancing worriedly toward the forest. It wasn't as if much time had passed, but it had been more than long enough to retrieve the ball.

"I guess he couldn't find it right away?" suggested Shoji.

The four remaining boys crossed the tree line, determined to help Tokoyami search, but he was nowhere to be found. Ida shouted for him.

"Tokoyami!"

"Over here."

They followed their friend's voice through the dense trees and found him staring at a certain spot on the ground.

"What's the matter?" asked Ida. Tokoyami raised his head and pointed down.

"My Dark Night...erm, the crystal stopped rolling here, but...the ground seems soft."

"Soft? How so?"

Ida moved toward Tokoyami as he spoke, and sure enough, that first step gave him confirmation. Not only was the ground soft, but it suddenly collapsed under Ida's weight, crumbling apart and swallowing the boys with an earth-shattering rumble.

"Wahhh?!"

"Hey... Hey! Wake up, fellas!"

"Hrm? Is that you, Dark Shadow...? Urgh."

Dark Shadow's voice had roused Ida, but when he tried to lift himself up, he groaned in reaction to the pain shooting across his back and arms. That's when he noticed how dark it was. Ida pushed the pain aside and fixed his askew glasses. How had they been transported from the forest to a dimly lit cavern, surrounded by walls of boulders?

Right, of course. The ground collapsed... Some sort of cave-in?

Ida realized he must have blacked out, so he shot up with a gasp and said, "Is everyone okay?!"

Dark Shadow had floated up to the top of a rock pile, where it was trying to wake up Koda. Nearby, a hardened Kirishima burst out of a pile of rocks and yelled, "Phew, thought I was a dead man!" Tokoyami and Shoji had also just opened their eyes, and their own pained grunts alerted one to the other. The boys confirmed that everyone else was relatively uninjured, and a relieved Ida began examining their surroundings.

The ceiling was an arch-shaped slab of stone, and it seemed that the hole they'd fallen through had been naturally plugged by rocks during the cave-in. It was hard to tell just how far they'd fallen, given the whole blacking-out thing. Since the cave was more than large enough to swallow up the massive quantity of rocks that had fallen in, Ida assumed that this hollowed-out space was responsible for the ground crumbling beneath their feet to begin with.

"Hey, hey! Check this out!"

The darkness had put some pep in Dark Shadow's step, and Tokoyami's shadowy familiar now pointed beyond some of the rocks. The boys fought past the aches and pains to stand up and investigate.

"What could that be...?"

Their eyes had begun to adjust to the darkness, but they didn't need night vision to see a string of red lights that seemed to burn, faintly. The lights led down a passage, like a beckoning trail of bloodstains, informing the boys that surely not everything about this space was entirely natural. In fact, when they got a closer look at the first red glow, they realized it was coming from a basic light bulb.

"Hmm?"

Alerted to the presence of intruders, a shadowy figure elsewhere adjusted a screen for a better look. The curious students had no idea that the lights that had captured their attention were in fact also capturing a live feed of them.

UA

The passageway illuminated by the faint red lights was broad and tall—about five meters across and three

meters high, so plenty large enough for an SUV to drive through. Despite the lights, the darkness was pervasive, and the boys couldn't see an end to the passage through the gloom. They could, however, see a number of off-shoot tunnels, each as wide as the main one. The walls appeared smooth from a distance, but a closer inspection revealed them to be coarse and rough-hewn.

"I never imagined such a cave structure existed beneath U.A.," murmured a stunned Ida. Kirishima gasped, as if he'd had an insight. "Maybe it's a new school facility?"

"That could explain it," said Shoji. Koda nodded in agreement.

"If they've been constructing this facility," said Tokoyami, "that would also explain the minor earthquakes and the sounds Shoji and Jiro have heard."

"Yes, in all likelihood," said Ida. The creeping unease brought on by the unfamiliar space was replaced with relief at this reasonable explanation.

"Let's explore, then!" yelped Dark Shadow, who'd been fidgeting and glancing around excitedly the entire time.

"No," said Ida, shaking his head. "As of this moment, we're victims of an accident. We ought to escape as soon as possible and... Ah, Tokoyami! Is your phone working?"

Tokoyami had indeed forgotten about his phone, but he yanked it from his pocket and made an attempt. His face quickly clouded over.

"No, I have no signal."

"Then we have no choice but to break free by our own power," stated Ida.

"Guess so," said Shoji. Koda nodded beside him.

"Let's freaking do this!" shouted Kirishima, as if he'd been waiting for an adventure to kick off.

"Indeed," added Tokoyami.

"Aw, 'break free'? What's the harm in exploring?!" whined Dark Shadow.

"If this is a new facility, then they'll probably schedule a visit for the class soon enough. Be patient," said Tokoyami, attempting to wrangle his unruly familiar. Meanwhile, Ida stared back at the ceiling they had fallen through.

"We have two potential means of escape," he began. "One: somehow remove the rocks that plugged the hole..."

"Or follow these paths and hope one of them leads back aboveground?" suggested Shoji.

"Makes sense," said Kirishima, surveying the massive underground space. "If someone's building this place, they've gotta have a way in and out."

"Yes, but we are without a proper map, and there's no telling how expansive these caves really are," said Ida.

"S'why we gotta explore!" said Dark Shadow, chiming in.

Which escape option seemed safer? As class president, Ida was duty bound to make proper decisions, but his thoughts were interrupted by a brassy clanging from deeper in the cave. The boys all spun around toward the source of the noise. Something small was moving in their direction. As it approached one of the red lights, the full form of a toy monkey with cymbals came into view. The group exchanged uneasy glances and walked over to the toy.

"The heck…?" said Kirishima, who—after a tense pause—hardened one hand and lifted the monkey. They all stared, waiting for something to happen, but the toy remained a toy. Nothing out of the ordinary.

"This little dude definitely wasn't chilling over here a minute ago, right?" asked Kirishima.

"Maybe it was just too dark for us to notice it," suggested Shoji.

"Why would such a contraption be here in the first place?" Ida wondered aloud.

Before anyone could answer, the monkey sprang to life and began smashing its tiny cymbals together with aplomb.

"Whoa!" yelped Kirishima, who dropped the toy in shock. The others flinched as well before chuckling in the silence that followed, perhaps out of embarrassment over their overblown reaction. Any shock on their part was soon justified, however, when the monkey's head spun around. Its eyes lit up, as if confirming targets, and a powerful beam aimed straight at the boys shot from its open mouth.

"Yikes!"

They narrowly avoided the point-blank attack, but the monkey—now somehow on its feet—wasted no time in firing off more beams.

"What's up with this?!" yelled a panicking Kirishima.

"Obviously I cannot explain it!" shot back Ida, whose fleet feet had put some distance between himself and the monkey.

"Get it, Dark Shadow!" shouted Tokoyami.

"Aye, aye!" replied the familiar, eagerly diving in to attack with claws and fangs bared. The dim surroundings neutered the beam blasts' range, but one close-up beam from the monkey hit Dark Shadow squarely in the eyes.

"Gahh!" it yelped, quickly shrinking back and retreating into Tokoyami's body.

"Dark Shadow!" cried Tokoyami, his voice wavering with concern.

Kirishima and Shoji were up next. The former's hardened body withstood the beam blasts without trouble, but as the duo moved within striking range, the monkey scampered off, so Shoji picked up a massive boulder and hurled it straight at the toy. When the dust had settled, the boys moved closer to make sure the target had been destroyed, but a good half of the monkey—including its head—was still intact. The toy's mouth popped open and closed.

"…*urse…urse…urse…*"

"Nurse...? How brazen, to request medical assistance from us at this point!" said Ida.

"I believe it's saying 'curse.' Like the sort involving voodoo dolls..." said Tokoyami.

Curse. The word hung in the air, and it slowly transformed the monkey into something far more sinister than it had seemed even a moment ago. Once again, the toy's mouth opened.

"Curse... Curse..."

They heard it clearly now, and it seemed obvious that the toy's creator had imbued it with malice and ill will. The boys gulped in unison. Under different circumstances, they might have laughed it off, but not in this dim, otherworldly space, where they were feeling quite down the rabbit hole already.

Suddenly the monkey's jaw popped open again, as if the head might split in two.

"Curse... Destroy!"

"Gahhh!"

The boys ran, but the mangled monkey toy floated into the air and pursued them.

"W-what now?!" shouted Kirishima.

"Don't ask me!" shot back Ida.

The solution might have been as simple as wrecking what remained of the toy, but the premise that it was cloaked in some invisible, unknowable curse made it all the more terrifying. Perhaps destroying it would curse them forever? Motivated by that primal instinct known as fear, the boys' every reflex was suddenly dedicated to escaping, but as they ran deeper into the tunnel, they were surprised to find more than just a few side passages. They saw countless openings, all evenly spaced apart. Still, it was all they could do to dodge the incoming beams from the pursuing toy.

"Any thoughts yet, Ida?!" asked Kirishima.

"First, we remove ourselves from its range, then wait for an opening, and..."

"Ida! Up ahead!"

Shoji's cry alerted Ida to an entire swarm of toy monkeys flying at the group from the other direction, all firing beam blasts.

"Whoa!"

They leaped down one of the side tunnels and were shocked to discover that this one had more branching paths of its own. They kept running, but dodging the curtain of beams was quickly becoming unfeasible.

"Ida, they're not stopping!" said Kirishima.

Still running, Ida considered their options before proposing a plan.

"You keep luring them ahead, Kirishima. Meanwhile, we shall conceal ourselves on either side."

Shoji and Tokoyami nodded in agreement and dove down a passage to the left while Ida ran to the right. Kirishima screeched to a halt, hardened his entire body to withstand the beam attacks, and took the opportunity to smash two or three of the toy monkeys with his rock-hard fists.

"Come and get me!" he shouted at the rest of the swarm before taking off running again.

Just as the monkeys flew past, the other three boys leaped out and attacked from behind, prompting Kirishima to once again spin around, effectively catching the pursuers in a pincer move.

"Curse... Curse... Curse curse curse..."

"Arghh!"

A final string of curses echoed like death throes as the toys were destroyed for good. Any hypothetical fear of invoking the curse by fighting back had been overshadowed by the much more tangible fear of the omi-

nous talking monkey toys. Having satisfied both their flight and fight instincts, the boys heaved sighs of relief.

"Seriously, what was their deal...?" asked Kirishima.

"I would very much like to know as well," said a scowling Ida, no better equipped to answer Kirishima's third such query than the first two.

"Is Dark Shadow doing okay?" asked Shoji.

"Yes... Any damage will be healed after a short rest," said Tokoyami.

"Wonderful to hear," said Ida, but his relief was soon replaced by the sense that something was off.

"Where is Koda?"

The other three hadn't realized their classmate was missing until that moment. They shouted for Koda, but the only answer was their own echoes. Even the ears on Shoji's dupli-arms couldn't detect any trace of their classmate.

"Perhaps he became separated earlier as we fled?" suggested Ida.

They tried retracing their route back to their starting point, but the pile of rubble that had marked the spot where they'd fallen was nowhere to be found.

"Huh?" said Kirishima. "It was definitely here, yeah?"

"No, I think it was that way," said Shoji.

"I believe that was the way we came from," said Tokoyami.

Each of the three pointed in different directions, and realizing that, they grimaced at what seemed to be a bad omen.

"Please don't tell me...that we've lost our way as well?!"

The tinge of panic in Ida's voice was apparent. The many side tunnels they'd observed earlier revealed just how convoluted and enormous this underground space really was.

"What's our course of action, Ida?" asked Tokoyami.

"We search for both Koda and the exit."

U A

"Gimme back my lint roller, Kirishima... Wait, huh?"

Katsuki Bakugo, who had nearly finished his cleaning, stopped by Kirishima's room. He was none the

wiser that his friend was at that moment battling it out in the underground dungeon.

"How long's it take to trash a freakin' punching bag?"

With his usual grumbles, Bakugo barged into his friend's room and found the lint roller he'd come to collect sitting on the floor. As he clucked his tongue in annoyance and bent over to pick up the tool, he noticed a prominent dust clump under the bed.

"Y'call *that* clean?"

The skilled kid known as "the Talented Mr. Bakugo" to his classmates was, needless to say, a pro at tidying as well, so it barely took him a second to swipe at and extract the dust with the long-handled lint roller. Bakugo stood up with a derisive snort and then noticed a torn poster on the verge of ripping off the wall, hanging near other pieces of paper on which Kirishima had written inspirational phrases.

"Whatcha doing in Kirishima's room?"

Hanta Sero had also been dropping by to borrow Bakugo's lint roller, and as he'd passed Kirishima's doorway, he'd found Bakugo busy rehanging the poster.

"When Kirishima hung up those weird papers, he somehow ripped this poster, so I'm fixing it. Duh."

That was obvious enough, but what Sero wanted to know was why this task had fallen to Bakugo in particular. Before he could rephrase, though, he noticed Bakugo managing the job with dexterity and guessed that Kirishima's half-assed cleaning hadn't sat well with the meticulous Bakugo.

"Y'know, Bakugo," said Sero. "If, against all odds, the whole hero thing doesn't pan out, you could totally start an odd-jobs shop."

"Huh?! There's no universe where that happens!"

U A

While Bakugo was roaring at Sero, Kirishima and the others were busy staring at a wall. They'd been cautiously creeping down passages in their search for Koda, but the pathways had kept branching until they had no clue where they were or where to go next. Finally, they hit a dead end, but attached to the wall was a strange button that seemed to scream, "Push me!" It was as if the simple protrusion was enchanted to draw in passersby and fill them with an inescapable desire to push it.

"Should we?" asked Kirishima, unable to hide his childlike curiosity. The others felt the same way, but Ida resisted and shook his head.

"We haven't the faintest what pushing this button could do!" he said.

"But it might alert the ones running the facility to the danger we're in. Pushing it could get us rescued," suggested Tokoyami.

"Assuming this really is a U.A. facility."

Shoji's words of doubt—spoken cautiously, since he was the first to bring up the idea—were met with silence. Ida had secretly been thinking the same thing.

"I have my doubts as well," he said. "A mazelike training facility is certainly within the realm of possibility, but I cannot explain the toy monkeys. Even if they were meant to represent villains, why unleash them before construction was completed?"

"But if it's not connected to U.A., then…" murmured Tokoyami. The other three finished his thought under their breaths, in unison.

"Villains…"

A dark pall fell over the group, but Kirishima forced a smile in an attempt to smash the bad vibes.

"C'mon, though—how would villains create a huge place like this without anyone noticing?" he said.

"I shudder to think villains could be behind this," said Ida, "though we'd be remiss not to consider the possibility."

As the four boys carried on with their grave conversation, Dark Shadow slowly emerged from Tokoyami, having recovered from the earlier damage. Still wary of the monkey beams, it glanced around nervously. Tokoyami ignored his familiar for the moment—rather than interrupt the serious talk of potential villains—but this proved to be a mistake.

"Ooh, what's this?" said the curious Dark Shadow, pushing the mystery button without an ounce of hesitation.

"Argh!"

"Dark Shadow! What have you done?!" shouted Tokoyami.

Dark Shadow had no idea why the boys were gasping in horror and freaking out.

"Please! Remain calm!" said Ida.

"If villains really are to blame for all this, they might've set traps..." said Shoji, who had wasted no

time in scanning their surroundings for impending danger.

"Sure, like in the movies," said Kirishima. "In this kinda sitch, the first trap is usually a trapdoor..."

They glanced at the ground and noticed a nearly imperceptible seam.

"Everyone, to the wall!" shouted Ida, fearing a sudden pitfall. The others obeyed, slamming their backs to either side of the dead-end tunnel. But the ground showed no sign of splitting open. As the group peered at the suspicious seam, Ida felt a bit of crumbling dirt fall on his head and glanced up just in time to see the ceiling rushing toward them.

"Everyone! Run!"

"Huh? Ack!"

Ida's timely alert had kept them from being crushed by a two-meters-square block falling from the ceiling, but before they had a moment to breathe, another block was descending upon their new position.

"What nowww?!" yelled Kirishima as the chain of blocks began falling faster and faster. Shoji, running at the back of the group, had a leg grazed by one of the weighty death traps. Meanwhile, after confirming that

Tokoyami had cloaked himself with Dark Shadow and was using his Black Fallen Angel mode to fly down the tunnel, Ida slowed down just enough to grab Shoji's and Kirishima's hands.

"Here we go, you two!"

"Whoaaa?!"

The three boys blasted down the tunnel at a ferocious speed, courtesy of Ida's "Engine" Quirk. Within seconds, the falling blocks were far in their rear view, and after another moment, they'd moved a safe enough distance away to pump the brakes.

"You saved us... I've never moved quite that fast before..." said Shoji, gasping for breath.

"Felt like we turned into a gust of wind, there..." added Kirishima, also panting.

Ida apologized for the impromptu escape tactic and breathed a sigh of relief when at last the sound of falling blocks had subsided.

"Yes, we seem safe for now," continued Ida. "And clearly that button was indeed linked to a trap."

"Let's hope it's the last one we trigger."

"Wanna do it again!" chirped Dark Shadow, treating the death trap like a ride at a carnival. As Tokoyami

glanced upward to scold his floating familiar, he noticed a monitor attached to the ceiling. One completely out of place in the rocky environs.

"What is that screen doing here?" he said.

As he spoke, a "10" flashed on the monitor. The other three boys were now paying attention as the monitor displayed "9" and then "8."

"What is it counting down to...?" said Ida.

Countdowns are one way to exert control over human psychology. They inspire both a sense of caution and excitement, driving the viewer to stick around and see what happens at the end. This countdown had the boys in its grasp, drawing their eyes while also causing them to back away instinctively. When it reached "0," the much-discussed trapdoor flapped open beneath them.

"Wahhh?!"

They had been standing directly over the pitfall that lay in wait, so there was no hope of grabbing onto the edge or otherwise stopping their descent. Nor could they resist zooming down the convenient slide placed directly below, which had been slicked over with some kind of oil in preparation for just for this very moment. As they slid down in the darkness, any attempts to right themselves only got them more tangled up, to a comical extent.

"Ida, your exhaust pipe thing's taking a trip up my butt!" said Kirishima.

"Apologies. Allow me to... Ouch! What just stabbed the back of my head?!"

"Dah muh eek!" mumbled a muffled Tokoyami, attempting to explain that it was his beak drilling into Ida's head, though his explanation was drowned out by Ida's pained cries. Meanwhile, Shoji was at the head of the pack. When the other three slammed into his back, he tried to peel them away but only managed to get his own arms tangled up in the flailing ball of limbs. The four boys' combined weight shot them down the greased slide with more momentum than ever, and the slide shifted to a near-vertical drop, until...

Freefall.

"Ahhhh!"

The boys were rendered speechless for a moment by the jarring sensation of their stomachs floating around in their bodies, but they managed to gasp when they saw what awaited them at the bottom of the fall.

A lattice of iron bars, shaped into a giant birdcage. The top was popped open and seemed ready to slam shut the instant that unwitting victims fell in. Imprisonment seemed inevitable, especially since their greased-up bodies had no means by which to resist. Just before falling into the cage, however, the boys suddenly found themselves floating back up.

"I! Hate! Birdcages!" grunted Dark Shadow, holding all four aloft. The boys' eyes sparkled as they beheld their savior—a dark angel incarnate.

"Well done, Dark Shadow!" said Tokoyami.

"Keep the praise coming!"

Having cleared the birdcage's yawning opening, they landed a short distance away in a nearby tunnel. Unlike the other passages, this one had no offshoots and seemed to slope downward. Not ready to move on just yet, the group slumped to the ground in a circle.

"So many intricate traps," said Ida. "All designed to capture intruders such as ourselves. I'm hard-pressed to believe that this is truly a U.A. facility."

"This labyrinthine trap hoard seems more like something constructed by villains," said Tokoyami.

"Y'think...the villains are in here with us?" suggested Kirishima.

"There's a good chance they're somehow watching us, at least," said Shoji.

"Regardless, our objective remains the same. Find Koda, and find the exit. Then, we report back to Aizawa Sensei and inform him about our discovery!" concluded Ida.

The thought that villains were once again taking aim at U.A. from the shadows lit a fire in the hearts of these four, who could very well be the only ones aware of the plot at the moment. They were inspired to fight back.

"I hope Koda is unharmed... We've traveled quite a bit since losing him," said Ida.

"We can only hope that the villains haven't caught him," said Tokoyami, assuming the worst.

But Ida took control of his own panicked thoughts, stood up, and said, "Let's press onward."

Suddenly there came an enormous slam from behind. Several paces away, a perfectly round boulder had dropped—one that seemed an exact fit for the breadth of the tunnel. Succumbing to gravity, it slowly began rolling down the slope.

"No way... Nuh-uh! We've gotta be on a movie set, right?" shouted Kirishima.

"Sadly, Kirishima, I'm afraid this is reality!" said Ida as the boys ran from the boulder, which was already picking up speed. The slope's slant grew sharper, and just as the old cliché would have it, they spotted a dead end ahead. With nowhere left to run, Kirishima found the resolve to spin around, plant his feet, and shout.

"We'll see who breaks first!"

Kirishima's whole body hardened up, and behind him, the other three braced themselves for impact.

"We have your back, Kirishima! Get the job done!" said Ida.

With Ida's cheer encouraging him, Kirishima thrust his fists at the spinning boulder, just barely managing to withstand a force that would've crushed a lesser man. Small cracks spread across the boulder's surface and quickly blossomed into massive fissures that tore the raging rock in two. A fully prepared Ida leaped at one half with a kick, while Shoji smashed the other half with his Octoblow assault. A splintered piece of rock bounced off the wall and flew toward Tokoyami, however, who was caught off guard and couldn't react in time.

"Ugh!"

Ida winced, having taken a direct hit to the shoulder while shielding Tokoyami.

"Oh no, Ida!" said Tokoyami, gasping as his face crumpled. Kirishima and Shoji also ran over to their injured friend.

"That's blood, dude!" said Kirishima.

"Let's try to stop the bleeding," said Shoji, but before he could tear off a strip of his own clothing, Ida pulled out a handkerchief from his pocket and said, "Please—use this." The wound was dressed with the handkerchief, but blood began oozing right through it.

"Apologies!" said Tokoyami, clenching his fists in frustration, but Ida forced a smile past the pain.

"It's just a scratch, so don't let it trouble you. Besides, we haven't the luxury to fritter away our time sitting here..."

Ida stumbled a bit from the pain. Tokoyami was ready to assist, but when his hand accidentally grazed the bloody wound site, he flinched and ripped his hand away to stare at it.

"I'm so sorry..." he said. "This is my fault!"

Tokoyami typically presented himself as an aloof loner, but on the inside, he actually cared about his friends a great deal. When the League of Villains had attacked the class during the forest training camp, Shoji had been hurt shielding Tokoyami from an attack, and the latter had then lost control over his emotions, leading to Dark Shadow's monstrous rampage. Then and now, in situations where darkness was more prevalent than light to begin with, Tokoyami's heart was primed to snap. In turn, Dark Shadow grew larger and more ferocious in response to these heightened emotions.

"The dark is my domain! Lemme go wild!" it roared.

"Enough, Dark Shadow..." pleaded Tokoyami as his familiar loomed over the boys, with the dead end at their backs. Tokoyami struggled, but in the darkness, Dark Shadow reigned supreme. Ordinarily, it was like class 1-A's lovable little sibling—friendly, chatty, and reliable in a pinch—but the darkness had a way of throwing off Dark Shadow's shackles, turning it into a powerful beast prone to attacking friend and foe alike. If Tokoyami himself couldn't rein it in through force of will, then a flash of light was their best hope.

MY HERO ACADEMIA SCHOOL BRIEFS

"Light… Of course," murmured Ida. "Lend me your cellular phone, Tokoyami!"

He reached into Tokoyami's pocket and grabbed the phone, hoping to use the flashlight function to weaken Dark Shadow, but before he could aim the light properly, the monster's sweeping claws smacked the phone out of Ida's hands and knocked it against the wall.

"Dun need light!"

Intent on eliminating any threats to its existence, Dark Shadow bared its fangs at the boys, ready to strike. But then Shoji gasped.

"Something's coming!"

Ear-piercing screeches. The flapping of wings. A swarm large enough to block the width of the tunnel. A close encounter with more black creatures that thrived in darkness.

"Bats?"

The countless bats swallowed up Dark Shadow, as if to shield the stupefied boys.

"Gah!" yelped Dark Shadow, as Tokoyami's jaw dropped.

Suddenly, they heard a familiar voice amid all the flapping.

"Yes, surround that dark, shadowy creature."

"Koda!"

"Calm yourself, dark one," implored Koda as he used his "Anivoice" Quirk to command the swarm of bats.

"Batboy!" said Tokoyami, his eyes practically sparkling with adulation. As Tokoyami's own spirit was calmed, Dark Shadow seemed to come to its senses.

"But I'm way cooler than Batboy!" it shouted, shrinking down to its normal size before Tokoyami shoved it back into his body. Koda sighed with relief, thanked the bats, and released them from his control. The other four ran to him.

"We were about to be Dark Shadow chow, so thanks!" said Kirishima.

"We've been searching for you!" said Ida. "Where on earth were you?"

"Well, you see…"

Koda explained that after getting separated from the group, he'd fallen through a trapdoor and gotten horribly lost. However, the bugs and bats in the area had helped lead him to this spot.

"Koda... I must thank you for stopping Dark Shadow. What a powerful Quirk you have," said Tokoyami, the admiration apparent in his voice and eyes.

"Really? I dunno..." said Koda, who couldn't help but blush and smile sheepishly.

The celebration was cut short by the appearance of a giant hose near the tunnel entrance. Water began gushing out, and within seconds, the boys were underwater. Fortunately, the dead-end wall rumbled, shook, and shifted open.

"Wahhh!"

The torrent of water—desperate to find an outlet—rushed through the opening, dragging the five boys with it. They flipped, flopped, spun, and plummeted down the impromptu waterslide. Not wanting to lose anyone again, Ida reached out toward Tokoyami and Kirishima, but the chaotic current prevented him from grasping their hands. It was all they could do to keep their heads above water, until Shoji grabbed each of the other four and pulled them over to his back.

"Grab ahold!"

"Thanks, Shoji!"

His broad back gave them some degree of protection and reminded each of them of a parental figure's back that had made them feel at ease when they were children.

At last the instant river deposited them into the most enormous tunnel yet. They slowly regained feeling in their sopping, chilled bodies and started to tremble. The cold couldn't stop them now, though. They marched onward and began to warm up.

"Anyone else suddenly feeling toastier?" asked Kirishima.

"Yes, though I couldn't tell you why," said Ida.

While the gang wondered about the temperature change, Tokoyami noticed puffs of steam coming from the other side of the area. Rushing to the source, they discovered a large underground hot spring. Kirishima tested the water with one hand.

"Yep, that's steamy..."

A hot spring conveniently available for their frozen bodies? It was hardly an offer they could refuse. They poked around a bit more and found a changing area that for some reason was furnished with five tracksuits and five towels. It seemed increasingly unlikely that vil-

lains would have provided all this, including a tracksuit that looked like it would perfectly fit Shoji's large and unique body.

"It's hard to imagine that any villain would be quite so hospitable," said Ida.

"Right...?" agreed Kirishima.

It was definitely suspicious, but the boys decided to take advantage of the hot spring, making sure that someone was keeping watch at all times. As they slipped into the water and relaxed, they realized how utterly exhausted they were. And though it weighed on their consciences a bit, they decided to use the towels and tracksuits after all. Ida and Koda were the last to emerge from the hot spring, and a flustered Shoji returned from scouting just as they were changing into their new outfits.

"This way, guys! Quickly!" he said.

The other four followed Shoji to a passageway lined with impressive metal doors that looked out of place in an earthen tunnel. They approached one of the doors, and Shoji whispered, "I hear people in there."

"Huh?" blurted out Kirishima loudly before clapping his hands over his mouth.

At Shoji's signal, they all moved toward the door gingerly and placed their ears against it.

"So when's this operation going down?" came a voice.

"Ain't it obvious? Right freakin' now! We're gonna do some real damage, I tells ya!" said another.

The boys gasped and turned to each other. Not only were their suspicions confirmed—villains really had built this place—but the villains in question were about to launch a full-scale attack on U.A. There would be dire consequences if they couldn't escape and tell the teachers, but that was easier said than done, considering the scope of this subterranean labyrinth. That left them with one other option—confronting the villains on their own.

Without speaking a word, each knew what the others were thinking, and all five nodded in unison. Even Dark Shadow emerged to pitch in.

"Dark Shadow, bring the door down!" whispered Tokoyami.

"Aye, aye!"

The metal door looked as sturdy as anything, but powerful blows from Kirishima and Dark Shadow smashed it inward without trouble, and all five boys

leaped into the room, prepared for battle. But they found nobody to fight.

"My poor Suprah… We're gonna hit 'em back ten times as hard for keying my baby!"

"For sure. Let's send their precious Fairlady X to the boneyard!"

"Don'tcha mean the scrapyard, ya numbskull?"

"Huh?"

The confused boys found themselves staring at a projection screen that showed a car covered in scratch marks and surrounded by a gang of supremely ticked-off looking hoodlums. The scene happened to be from *Ridge Racers: Righteous Car Crusade*, a C-tier cult movie that nobody outside of the niche fandom had ever heard of, least of all these high school boys.

"Is this…a small movie theater…?" wondered Ida aloud, as he and the others glanced around.

It certainly seemed to be. The impressive screening room had about thirty seats and was equipped with a state-of-the-art speaker system to create the perfect ambiance. Tokoyami finally spoke up and voiced the question on all their minds.

"Why would villains build a movie theater…?"

Movie theaters were made for entertaining, and this simple fact only enhanced their confusion.

"Sorry…" said Shoji, apologizing for mistaking the movie characters for villains.

"An understandable error," said Ida. "Though it would seem there are no villains in our immediate environs after all."

"Should we check out some of the other doors?" asked Kirishima.

They agreed and approached another door. This one wasn't locked, so they opened it gingerly using the actual doorknob.

"This one appears to be someone's room," was Ida's succinct assessment, and the others nodded. There was a leather sofa and a desk with a half-drunken mug of coffee and an instant ramen container. Posters of cars were plastered up on the walls, offering a glimpse at the inhabitant's interests. It was indeed someone's personal quarters, plainly and surely.

"Y'think someone's living down here?" asked Kirishima with a tilt of his head.

They tried the next door, which was also unlocked, allowing them to slip right in. They were shocked to

discover that this chamber contained an entire full-size racetrack and a number of classic cars. Ida suddenly realized the common factor between the contents of the chambers.

"This villain seems to be a car lover! A gearhead, if you will!"

This wasn't a particularly useful nugget of information, so they made a mental note and proceeded to the next room, which was a workshop crammed full of machines, half-built robots, weapon-like objects, and devices whose purposes evaded conjecture altogether. The boys crept around and inspected each baffling machine with suspicious scowls on their faces.

"They seem to be producing weapons in here?" said Shoji.

"Maybe this entire underground lair is the villains' home base," added Tokoyami.

"No freaking way!" said Kirishima, whose red alert senses had just kicked into high gear. Koda also fidgeted and began to show signs of panic. After a moment of tense thought, Ida made his assessment.

"If they truly possess the resources to construct a facility of this scale, unbeknownst to U.A., then I'm afraid we're dealing with a band of well-prepared, terrifyingly brazen, low-down and dirty villains!"

An unsteady pile of inventions collapsed, and one malfunctioning machine popped out of the heap, moving erratically. Somehow it managed to activate some of the other devices before taking aim at the boys with plumes of weaponized fire.

"Holy cow!"

They dodged the flames, but the chain reaction wasn't slowing down. Some of the machines leaped around the room with deadly momentum, some fired laser beams, some emitted blinding flashes of light, and still others launched bevies of mini missiles, all contributing to the utter chaos. Was it a villain attack? Or merely malfunctioning machines? Ida didn't have a spare moment to mull over the question, so he shouted the only order he could.

"We have to stop them!"

They fought back as best they could given the turmoil, figuring that the only way to stop the machines from activating others was to wreck each one within reach. When the last rampaging device was destroyed, a small figured appeared behind them.

"Hello, boys."

"Principal?"

Yes, the adorable, diminutive mammal standing in the doorway was none other than Principal Nezu—the head honcho at U.A. High. The scar over his right eye ran counter to his otherwise charming appearance, giving him an air of someone with a darker past than he tended to let on. In any case, the five boys instinctively rushed over to Nezu, whose presence was immediately reassuring.

"We have grave news to report!" blurted Ida. "We seem to have stumbled upon a villain lair!"

Ida went on to explain the tale—from their accidental fall until that very moment—while the other four chimed in to support his story and insist that this was an emergency of the highest order.

"Quite a day you've had, indeed. But rest assured, this is no villain hideout," said Nezu.

"Huh?"

The boys were visibly confused, so Nezu spread his hands wide and went on.

"This entire place is actually an old U.A. facility!"

"H-huhh?"

"We planned to create a survival training facility underground," he explained, "but in the end, we deemed it too dangerous and sealed it off. The ground above must have weathered over time, leading to your unorthodox entry into the maze. I'm so very sorry you were exposed to these dangers."

"That's quite all right," said Ida, with a robotic bow. "I'm only sorry we jumped to such a hasty and erroneous conclusion!"

Ida may have been convinced, but Tokoyami still had questions.

"What about the room with the sofa, though? There was evidence that someone had been in there not long before we came by."

"Ah, that," said Nezu. "I've been down here recently, assessing whether or not the entire facility should be demolished, and that has been my break room, so to speak. So much assessing to be done, you see. Now then, let's put this place behind us on the double, and I'll have your clothes sent back to the dorm later."

Principal Nezu's familiar smile was enough to convince the boys, although he did make them promise not to speak a word of what had happened to anyone.

They followed his precise directions down the tunnels and came upon an elevator, which brought them aboveground and to another door.

But instead of trees and sunlight, a sort of staging room was waiting for them on the other side. More half-built machines. A wall calendar featuring cars. They couldn't help but wonder why the dungeon exited into such a place, but they pushed the question aside and stepped out into a hallway within the main school building.

Nezu had given them permission to visit the nurse's office, so after a quick trip to Recovery Girl (who healed Ida's wound), they finally emerged outside, where their euphoric sense of liberation was enough to clear their minds of any small doubts or misgivings. It was already evening, and the sky was shifting from mellow shades of orange to deeper blues. Feeling the cool breeze against their skin, the boys breathed deeply and stretched.

"I gotta say, that was kinda fun, right?" said Kirishima, smirking like a naughty schoolboy and looking to the gang for validation.

Tokoyami, Koda, and Shoji nodded, not nearly as grumpy as they had every right to be. Ida, however, spun his arms wildly and countered.

"One wrong step and our misadventure could have ended in tragedy!"

"I'm sorry," said Tokoyami, remembering Ida's injury. "You were hurt on my account..."

"Yes, but, that is to say..." blurted a flustered Ida, clearly embarrassed, before finding the resolve to speak his mind.

"I suppose I had a bit of fun as well. It was a grand adventure for the ages."

He and Tokoyami exchanged awkward smiles. The other three also smiled as they watched the exchange play out, until Koda's stomach began to grumble. He gripped his midsection as if to suppress the noise while the others chuckled.

"Tonight, we shall feast on hamburgers!" declared Ida with a grin as wide as any.

As the boys ran back to their dorm sweet dorm, Principal Nezu was still underground, surveying one of the rooms with an air of exasperation. This was a room the unwitting intruders hadn't stumbled into, filled with even more mountains of machines than the other workshop. Nezu sensed someone approaching from behind and spun around.

"Unbelievable... Did you have to make this place quite so labyrinthine, Power Loader?"

"Sorry, boss..."

The earnest apology came from Power Loader—the shirtless Support Course teacher who went around wearing a steam shovel helmet. In his hand, he clutched a device that alerted him to intruders in the maze.

Principal Nezu's explanation to the boys had been an outright lie. In truth, Power Loader had been at his wit's end about what to do with Mei Hatsume's inventions (or "babies," as she called them), which had started to overflow the Support Course workshop she'd made into her home away from home. When he'd brought up the issue with Nezu, the principal had suggested carving out an underground storage chamber. Once the project had begun, however, Power Loader had started enjoying himself a little too much, eventually constructing a room of his own, a racetrack for the cars he loved so much, and a cozy home theater.

When he'd struck metaphorical gold and unearthed a natural hot spring, Power Loader had come up with the idea to expand the project into a subterranean survival dungeon for the students' benefit, which had led him to excavate just a bit too close to the surface. That was where Ida and the boys had fallen through the ground, of course. Meanwhile, the beam-firing toy monkeys were an invention of Hatsume's—designed to train heroes to overcome fear—and the towels and such in the changing room had been sneakily placed by Power Loader himself, who didn't want the hapless boys catching cold in the dank underground space.

"The home theater, the racetrack, the hot spring... This wonderland is wasted on you alone... Oh, I know! Why not make these facilities available to all the staff, as a means of R&R?" suggested Nezu.

"Erm… I suppose, but…" stammered Power Loader, at a loss for words. Nezu observed this reaction carefully before chuckling.

"Just kidding, of course!"

"Huh?"

"I'm well aware that socializing is hardly your forte. I place a high value on camaraderie among my staff, but I would never force an introvert out of his comfort zone. We all need our personal space, don't we?"

It was all true—as an eccentric genius type, Power Loader was something of a loner who found it difficult to be around others. He definitely kept his colleagues at arm's length, but it wasn't out of dislike. Cementoss was an occasional conversation partner, since the two men often worked on construction projects together, but for the most part Power Loader regarded the other teachers as work friends, which was enough. He found much more meaning in time spent communing with machines, which maintained an irreplaceable position in his life. Principal Nezu understood this well.

"A mind like yours requires time and space to work on projects, yes? And this isolated space allows you to devote yourself to that work without interference."

As Nezu spoke, he toddled over to one of the piles of machines, which happened to be the accumulation of Power Loader's prototype support items.

"Thank you, sir," said Power Loader, forcing the words out. "But fooling the boys like that... It's kinda not in a human way."

"Heh heh...you think so? Just as well, since I'm not human at all."

Power Loader chuckled at his boss's little joke. Despite being an animal, Nezu's mind operated at a higher level than that of most people, so these two geniuses understood each other all too well.

"I know what it's like to get caught up in the excitement and take matters too far, but you'll have to implement better safety protocols for this underground dungeon if you don't want me to rescind my permission. Everything in moderation!"

"Yes, sir," said Power Loader, slumping his shoulders.

"That said, expect me to visit your hot spring from time to time," added Nezu.

UA

Only a select few individuals know of the underground dungeon beneath U.A. High.

If ever a day comes when another ragtag group of students falls into the dungeon, the experience will be sure to fluster them, encourage growth, and deepen friendships. Until that day, however, the labyrinth slumbers, providing only an odd bit of rest and relaxation for those in the know.

It was a wall-to-wall packed house in the tiny, intimate venue. From offstage, Kyoka Jiro watched her father beat the drums and her mother play guitar while belting out vocals. Kyotoku and Mika worked in the music industry, but this New Year's Eve performance was more of a personal side gig for them. Since the students of 1-A had just been granted permission to go home for the holiday, Kyoka was able to be in attendance.

The deep, pounding drums rattled her guts, and the guitar wailed like a diva. Kyoka's body internalized the rhythm instinctively; it came as naturally as breathing to her, since she'd been raised in such a musical family. The spirited crowd had also given itself over to the music and was clearly having a blast. Suddenly, Kyoka remembered she hadn't come alone, and she spun around.

"Not too loud for you I hope, Ectoplasm Sensei?"

For these home visits, a pro hero had been assigned to each student as a bodyguard.

"Not at all. As a first timer, I find it refreshing and intriguing," said her teacher.

"Want to join me over here, then? Your view can't be great from back there."

"May I really? If you insist..."

Ectoplasm moved closer to Kyoka and tried to find the rhythm again, though he was perpetually off the beat. His bumbling awkwardness brought a smile to Kyoka's face.

"The patrons appear to be enjoying the show. But perhaps this warranted a larger venue?" said Ectoplasm, observing the cramped crowd.

"Well, this little club has some sentimental value since it's where my parents met. So they play here every New Year's," explained Kyoka.

"I see. How inconsiderate of me to make such a suggestion, in that case."

Kyoka smiled and shook her head as if to say, "Don't sweat it," before turning back and letting the music take her over again. The rhythm and melody formed the pulse of her life. Not only did music come as naturally as breathing to her—it felt just as vital. Even more so when she relinquished control and allowed herself to meld with the sounds. A moment later, Kyotoku was amping up the crowd and prepping them to start the big countdown to midnight.

Crud. What'm I gonna do for my kakizome *homework?*

Kyoka's mind abruptly turned to the winter break homework from Aizawa Sensei, which was the traditional calligraphy drawn with an ink brush to usher in the New Year—ranging from a single kanji character to a phrase to an entire poem. More specifically, the assignment was to express an aspiration for the coming year. Naturally, Kyoka intended to tackle the year with the usual Plus Ultra spirit, but putting that sentiment into calligraphy was a little tricky.

"Happy New Year, everyone! Let's rock this year!"

Kyoka winced with a grin at her father's unabashed shouting, and her parents—still onstage—turned to her and winked. Kyoka didn't know what to make of this, but her father soon made it very clear.

"And now, you lucky folks get to hear from a first-time guest performer... Our daughter, Kyoka!"

"Huh?"

Kyoka was frozen in place, watching her parents' beckoning hands. They hadn't mentioned that she was slated to be part of the show, so her immediate response to the surprise invitation was to shake her head in fervent refusal.

"Our daughter can be a little shy. Hang on, folks," said Kyotoku. He and Mika walked offstage and were greeted by Kyoka's whispered protests.

"How about a little warning!" she hissed.

"Please, Kyoka?" said her mother. "You sang at the School Festival, didn't you?"

"Uh, yeah! And I sent you the recording!" said Kyoka.

"Which was great!" said her father. "But of course we wanna hear you live too!"

Kyoka couldn't bring herself to let them down, given how earnest they were about it. In fact, a part of her had wished they could've seen her big moment at the festival in person.

"Fine. Same song, though," declared Kyoka, finding the resolve deep in her gut. Her parents gave her a big hug, and the three members of the Jiro family strode out onto the stage together, where Kyoka introduced herself to the audience as quickly and awkwardly as possible. Then, with her parents providing accompaniment, she started to sing the song that had slain at the School Festival.

Kyoka was proud of her parents, who'd always given her support and encouraged her to do what she wanted, how she wanted, so she imbued this familial performance with all her resolve and gratitude. The crowd roared.

"Such a lovely voice," murmured a delighted Ectoplasm, who was still in the wings. The karaoke-loving teacher had heard tales of Kyoka's fabulous performance at the festival and had quietly been hoping for a chance to hear her live. It hadn't taken long into the New Year for his wish to come true.

The final lyric left Kyoka's lips, and the crowd went wild with cheers and applause. She was still feeling bashful about the whole thing but managed to turn to smile at her parents, who beamed right back at her. That was when Kyoka realized what kanji character she wanted to write for the kakizome assignment. Her aspiration for the coming year would be represented by 響 (*hibiki*/*kyo*), meaning "sound," "reverberate," or "resonate." It also happened to be the first character in her first name—the *kyo* in "Kyoka."

Cuz my heart's gonna rock out so hard that those good vibrations bust down every obstacle this year throws at me. Even if Kaminari and Mineta will totally poke fun for using part of my own name.

Just as Kyoka had decided that anyone who dared to tease her would get a firsthand taste of her heart's mighty reverberations, the audience started shouting for an encore. Stunned, she glanced around and realized that Ectoplasm and her parents were egging her on too.

"Really?" said Kyoka. "O-okay, one more song, I guess."

It was now the New Year, and in that small music venue, the lovely diva's voice rang out, resonating with one and all.

Part 2
The Unlikeliest Santas

"And so, for the students' home visits on New Year's Eve, each will be accompanied by either one of you or another pro hero."

Principal Nezu spoke from within the warm and cozy confines of Shota Aizawa's neck wrapping, and the teachers of U.A. nodded in agreement. They were seated in the conference room for the staff meeting marking the end of the second school term, which meant that the teachers were just moments away from their own winter breaks.

The dormitory system had been implemented because the educators suspected there might be a mole at U.A. High. A series of information leaks had led them to guess that the League of Villains had somehow infiltrated the school, and keeping the students on campus at all times seemed like a decent way to smoke out the potential spy. There'd been zero suspicious activity for months, however, so Nezu had suggested that the students be allowed to spend New Year's with their families, at the very least.

The students hadn't balked about being forced into dorms; from the moment they'd gotten into U.A., they'd all been prepared to go the extra mile if it meant becoming heroes. Nevertheless, they were still high schoolers. No longer little kids, not yet adults, but rather somewhere within that brief interstice we call adolescence, hurtling toward the rest of their lives. There were times when they missed their parents dearly, and surely their parents occasionally felt the sting of empty-nest syndrome. The teachers had once been that age themselves, so they felt no reason to object to home visits for a single night.

"And on that note, let's assign guardians to students…"

Just as Nezu began speaking again, several of the teachers started to stand, thinking that "on that note"

signaled the end of the meeting. Realizing that they weren't free just yet, the would-be leavers sat back down with murmurs of "Sorry..."

"Really, now?" chided the principal. "How many escape attempts does that make?"

These particular teachers had prematurely risen from their chairs three times now.

"C'mon, we've all got, erm, plans and stuff! It's a real holy night, y'know!" said Present Mic, one of the usual suspects.

"I suppose I'm no match for an argument of that caliber," quipped Nezu sarcastically. "But even you, Aizawa? I'm shocked."

"I have to bring Eri to class A's Christmas party," said Aizawa, his usual listless expression changing not one iota. The name he spoke instantly lit up the room.

"Yes, how splendid!" said the principal. "Midoriya is a member of class A, yes? His presence will be sure to help that girl relax and enjoy herself."

"Little Eri has been looking forward to this party!" said Thirteen, beaming.

"And she's been wearing the Santa outfit that those kids gave her since the crack of dawn," added Midnight with a cheery smile. Present Mic and Vlad King were also grinning, and even Ectoplasm's mouth curved into a smile underneath his mask.

It had been a few months since Eri had begun living in the teachers' dorm, and by this point, her presence was like chicken soup for their souls. As educators, they were all rather fond of children to start with, and how could they not be moved by her tragic tale, her brave determination to accept her Quirk and move forward in life, her innocence and complete lack of guile?

Principal Nezu's beady eyes darted around the room at his staff, who were acting a bit like children themselves. But at the mention of the party Eri was so looking forward to, he decided to cut the meeting short and save the "Top Ten Morning Assemblies" presentation for another time. Though Nezu's heart wasn't quite human, it had still been won over by the little girl.

"On that note, let's bring this meeting to a close. You may decide who escorts which student based on geographic convenience. Dismissed."

The teachers chanted "Thank you, sir" in unison and began to stand.

"Ah, one more thing!" said Nezu, as he leaped out of Aizawa's collar. "Keep in mind that as of today, we've bolstered security measures..."

But his warning fell on distracted ears.

UA

"Where do I put my big sword?" asked Eri, staring with a furrowed brow at the absolute whopper of a sword in Aizawa's hands. They had just left class A's Christmas party, where she had randomly drawn Fumikage Tokoyami's contribution to the class gift exchange. Despite the look on her face, her voice was tinged with joy.

"Too dangerous near the door, cuz it might get knocked over," murmured Eri. "Maybe near my bed? But that could be really scary if it falls over at night when I'm sleeping."

The sword was longer than Eri was tall, and she knew it would be hard to keep it balanced and propped up. Aizawa decided to offer a suggestion.

"If you're not sure how to display it, I could hold on to it for you?"

Eri's jaw dropped for a second, but then she shook her head.

"Nuh-uh. It's my Christmas present."

Her apparent delight wasn't so much about the enormous sword itself, but rather the fact that she had gotten a present at all. Through that lens, it was only natural that the gift had to be displayed somewhere in her room.

"Right," said Aizawa, who instantly understood Eri's feelings based on the sparkle in her eyes.

"I dunno, though..." she said, looking up at the night sky. Seeing her face in profile like that led Aizawa to cast his gaze upward too. The winter sky was dotted with countless stars, all twinkling like little beads.

"Heh heh."

A chuckle burst from Eri.

"When Lemillion sees my big sword," she mused, "he's gonna be so surprised."

Visions of a gobsmacked Mirio Togata danced through Eri's head, and there was no trace on her face of the cloud that had once hung over her. As the ones who had rescued her and then some, Togata and Midoriya had played a massive role in helping her get to this point, emotionally. In fact, after losing his Quirk and

taking a leave of absence from classes, Togata had spent nearly every day with the girl. His effortless cheeriness had a way of spreading to everyone around him, and for Eri, who'd spent many a day locked away in the cold and dark, Togata embodied comfort, warmth, and safety. That sense of ease in the everyday was something every child needed.

"Feeling chilly?" asked Aizawa, noticing Eri's visible breath.

"Naw. Still all warm and steamy inside," she said. "And so full. That chicken was yummy! And the corn dog, and *takoyaki*, and fries…"

A bit of drool leaked from the corner of her mouth as she rattled off the list of delicacies from the party. When she realized, she hastily wiped the spit away.

"So full, but I guess I wanna eat more anyway," said Eri, sounding bashful about it.

She wasn't nearly as reserved as usual, perhaps owing to the excitement of her first-ever Christmas party. Eri was so talkative, in fact, that she had even gotten the tight-lipped Aizawa into a chatty mood.

"Which was the yummiest?" he asked.

"Like, number one? Hmm. Um... Everything was yummy... Oh, the big pretty cake too... But I liked the apple with chocolate best of all."

There had been a chocolate-fondue setup that invited partygoers to plunge pieces of fruit and marshmallows under the mini chocolate waterfall.

"It made me remember the candy apple that Deku made for me that one time," she added.

She was referring, of course, to the treat Midoriya had prepared for her during the School Festival, which was another variation on the "apple coated with something sweet" theme. Seeing Eri's smile once again, Aizawa couldn't help but grin a little. He knew that precious memories from childhood were sure to serve as protective shields later in life, so Eri would someday be all the better off with more such experiences backing her.

"Aizawa Sensei?" said Eri. "Will Santa visit Deku too?"

Aizawa was taken aback by the out-of-the-blue question. He mulled over how to answer for a beat, then spoke.

"That's up to Santa, I think."

Eri looked shocked for a second before seeming to accept—in a distinctly childlike way—that these mat-

ters were Santa's business and that was simply the way of things.

"I guess so," she said, nodding. A subtle shadow seemed to descend over her face, and her mouth opened and closed a few times as she struggled to put thoughts into words.

"What is it?" asked Aizawa.

"Will Santa visit me?"

Eri had learned so many things since coming to U.A. High—among them, the idea of seasonal holidays. Each came with events and customs of its own, which inevitably colored everyone's lives. Prepping for class A's Christmas party, for instance, had taught Eri about Santa Claus—the saintly figure who gave out gifts to children around the world. Ever since learning this delightful fact, she'd been wondering whether or not Santa would pay her a visit.

Still holding the sword, Aizawa crouched down to Eri's eye level.

"He absolutely will."

"Okay," said Eri, swallowing down any doubt she might have harbored with a nod and a gulp.

"Shall we?" said Aizawa, extending his hand.

"Uh-huh."

Eri gripped his hand, and the pair walked into the teachers' dorm building.

For a moment, the stars seemed to sparkle just a little brighter.

UA

'Twas the middle of the night before Christmas, and not a creature was stirring, least of all Eri.

Just outside her door, Aizawa approached Present Mic, who was already in position for this planned rendezvous.

"What on earth are you wearing?" hissed Aizawa, already looking exasperated.

Present Mic was decked out in a red hat with white fur trim, red coat and pants, black boots, and a fluffy white beard and mustache. Completing the costume was a white sack slung over his shoulder.

"I'm Santa Claus! Who else? Good of you to show up looking like you always do, though!" whispered Mic, pointing at Aizawa's usual black utilitarian garb.

The plan, of course, was to make a delivery to Eri from "Santa Claus." Mic had brought the idea to Aizawa, pointing out how tragic it would be if the excited girl didn't end up with a gift from Santa. Aizawa had been an overly rational child, so he'd stopped believing in Santa at a young age, but he saw no benefit to shattering the innocent fantasies of a little girl. Besides, even if Santa were real, he'd be bound to forget a few homes during his busy night, so why not take precautions? In that sense, it was only rational for the adults in Eri's life to bring her a present on behalf of Santa. After all, any good hero was duty bound to safeguard the dreams of children.

Aizawa suggested that just one of them sneak in the room to place the gift by her pillow, but his companion immediately rejected that idea.

"What if her eyes pop open and she just sees *you*? Then all of a sudden Santa's not real, and it's just some trinket from cruddy old Aizawa!" said Mic.

"You'd better not be planning to wake her," said Aizawa, casting a suspicious glare at Mic. Why would he don the whole outfit if he wasn't planning to show it to Eri?

"Hell naw! I'm talking 'bout keeping up the fantasy!" said Mic.

"Fine. What did you get her, anyway?" said Aizawa with a glance at the white sack. He'd been mocked for his awful fashion sense the last time he'd bought clothes for Eri, so he'd agreed to let Mic make this particular gift selection. Mic opened the sack and proudly revealed a box wrapped with a festive ribbon and topped with a bow.

"A deejaying set for kids!"

"Huh?"

"Don't gimme that skeptical look! This thing's way cooler than you'd think!"

The set looked simple enough to control but was otherwise the genuine article. Mic explained how allowing kids to have fun with music from a young age seemed important to him. Aizawa wasn't sure if this was up Eri's alley or not, but since he'd left the decision in Mic's hands, he gave a grunt of approval and reached for the doorknob.

"Come on. When I open the door, get in there quick and stay hidden."

"Let's go! Present time!"

Aizawa made eye contact with Mic and turned the knob, allowing the two men to slip inside the room. No sooner had they done so than they heard the window clack and the closet slide open.

"Huhh?"

Four overlapping voices.

Standing in the doorway, Aizawa and Mic saw Midnight crawling through the window and Thirteen emerging from the closet. Both women were decked out in their own Santa costumes. They all pointed at each other as if to say, "What are *youuu* doing here?"

"Hrm..."

A weak mumbling came from the bed as Eri stirred. The four educators scrambled to hide themselves in the darkness, stifling their breathing and masking their presences, like a quartet of ninja. They could imagine how the sight of three Santas and an Aizawa might confuse and fluster Eri, so they were determined not to get caught. Eri's undisturbed breathing resumed, and the teachers made eye contact. Escaping into the hallway would let in the light, which might wake up Eri, so instead they snuck into the bathroom.

Midnight Claus—with her sexy Santa miniskirt—was the last to squeeze into the bathroom since she'd taken a moment to close the window behind her.

"We're…a bit…cramped…" said Thirteen, who, with a Santa costume over her usual space suit and a white sack in her arms, actually took up more space than any of them.

"Scuse me!" said Midnight.

"Space Claus? Kind of a mishmash there, Thirteen!" said Mic.

"Actually, I think I resemble Santa Claus more than any of you," quipped Thirteen.

"True. She's got the 'plump and wide' angle down pat," said Midnight.

"I should've stuffed a pillow under my top, huh!" said Mic.

"Enough. Let's figure this out," hissed Aizawa, unwilling to indulge the others' nonsense.

"Fair enough," said Midnight, surveying the other three. "Seems to me that we all came to give Eri gifts from 'Santa,' right?"

"Yes," said Thirteen. "I planned this with some of our colleagues."

"Hang on, you mean everyone came up with the same idea?" asked Mic.

"We all wanted to put a smile on Eri's face, yes," said Thirteen, grinning under her helmet.

Eri brought a wholesome, healing energy to the teachers' dorm, so it was only natural that her new neighbors would want to keep her healthy, happy, and safe. Thirteen, in particular, had been looking after Eri each morning and at bath time. Initially, the girl had been reticent to ask for and accept help, but more recently she'd acclimated and gotten comfortable enough to even yawn loudly in Thirteen's presence. The way she immediately grew bashful in such moments was adorable enough to make Thirteen want to squeeze the girl and hold her tight.

"Exactly," said Midnight with a nod. In recent times, she had drawn pictures with Eri and read books to the girl when she couldn't sleep. When Eri called Midnight "Miss Art," the other teachers would poke fun at the goofy grin that arose on Midnight's face. Remembering those moments now had the same effect on her.

"Makes sense to me!" added Mic. He'd been teaching Eri the English alphabet the past few weeks, and hearing her sing the ABC song reminded him of why he'd become a pro hero and English teacher to start with. When Aizawa had told him that Eri was wavering between calling him "Mister English" and "Mister Mustache," Mic thought it was so cute that he'd broken out into an impromptu rap performance for Eri (which had only served to confuse her).

Aizawa agreed and nodded at his colleagues, who all turned to him and glared a bit.

"What did I do?" he asked, which only prompted deeper scowls.

"You're closest to Eri out of all of us," said Thirteen.

"Aren't you so special, Mr. Parental Figure!" said Midnight.

"S'not fair, man!" added Mic.

People, by nature, are bundles of desire. When someone else receives affection, they are inclined to desire that same affection. Aizawa's colleagues were jealous of Eri's fondness for him. Of course, given Eri's unfortunate circumstances, they never would've dreamed of pushing the issue in even a remotely aggressive way. They had to be the adults in the room, even if the situ-

ation irked their childish sides. Alas, even heroes were human.

Aizawa let loose an annoyed sigh as he realized that the grudge-filled glares were motivated by envy.

"Actually, Midoriya and Togata are closest to her," said Aizawa.

"Yeah, but out of all of us teachers! Anyhoo, I know my gift's gonna make that kid squeal with joy. That's gonna earn me some real vicarious brownie points, via Santa! Just call me Long Legs Claus!" crowed Mic.

Midnight and Thirteen glanced at each other.

"Well? What're you two giving her?" asked Midnight.

"A deejaying set for kids!"

Proud as ever, Mic went into a spiel about how great the gift was, but Midnight responded with a grin and a derisive snort.

"Oh yeah?" said Mic. "What's your awesome present, then?"

"I got her...a picture book," said Midnight.

"That's weirdly ordinary! I was totally expecting something risqué from you!"

"Ouch! Obviously not! Not until she's older, that is," said Midnight. "Besides, gifts are meant to delight the giftee, and when it comes to little kids, that means encouraging their favorite hobbies, no?"

"Ugh! Well, I say that kids oughta be exposed to all sorts of *new* experiences early in life! It's a great way to expand their potential later on, y'feel me? You're on my side, right, Thirteen?" said Mic.

"Um. I got her a teddy bear," said Thirteen.

"Is that what's been cramping our style?" said Mic, pointing at Thirteen's soft and squishy gift sack, which was taking up a huge amount of real estate in the center of the bathroom, pressing the teachers out to the sides.

"When I was young," said Thirteen, with a note of apology in her voice, "I loved giant stuffed animals."

Everyone present suddenly imagined an ecstatic Eri hugging a massive plushie. Picturing that perfect image, Mic gave a thumbs-up and said "Good going!" through clenched teeth. Midnight nodded as well.

"We'll have to take a picture of her with her new toy tomorrow," she said.

"Yes, let's!" added an exuberant Thirteen, fully caught up in the mood.

Aizawa didn't disagree that Eri would appreciate the stuffed animal, but then he snapped back to his senses

and remembered that they were chatting in a cramped bathroom in the middle of the night.

"Let's leave our gifts and be done with it. No reason to dawdle," he said.

"Okay!" said Mic with a start and a nod. "With a little teamwork, this mission will be complete in no time!"

"I don't think I've ever experienced such a meaningful, stimulating, and holy night," said Midnight.

"I have faith we can pull this off!" said Thirteen.

"Yeah!" said Aizawa's colleagues in unison.

All we're doing is putting presents on a pillow.

Aizawa kept this thought to himself because voicing the quip out loud would only make them quip back, and so on and so forth, effectively wasting more time.

The mission was as follows: to place the gifts near Eri's pillow without making a sound and leave the room undetected. After going over this ridiculously simple plan, Midnight peered out the cracked bathroom door, gave a signal, and opened it gently. Silently, the four teachers approached Eri's bed with bated breath, being careful not to knock over the giant sword leaning against the wall. As they peeked at her pillows, Aizawa noticed a charming angel figurine placed on the shelf attached to the headboard. He cocked his head, puzzled, since it wasn't a familiar sight.

Has she always had that thing?

The others, however, were too busy staring at the other angel—the one nestled all snug in her bed.

"Aww, deep in slumberland," said Midnight.

"Having pleasant dreams, hopefully," said Thirteen.

"Probably about Santa Cl—" said Mic, but he cut himself short. "Hang on—what's that next to her?"

When the others spotted the small sock on one of Eri's pillows, their faces clouded over. Eri must have been told that Santa filled stockings with presents, so she'd left out one of her own teeny-tiny socks. None of the gifts the four teachers had brought would fit inside, of course. Flustered, they scrambled away from the bed and toward the main door for an emergency conference.

"What now?" said Mic. "That little thing can't hold any of our awesome gifts!"

"It's fine. We'll just place the gifts near the pillow, as planned," said Aizawa.

"But if she wakes up to an empty sock, Eri will blame herself for not having prepared a larger one, no?" said Thirteen.

"I can picture that, yeah," said Midnight.

"Your book's the smallest gift we got, Midnight. Try cramming that in there!" said Mic.

"This jumbo-sized book? I very much doubt it," said Midnight.

"Where's your Plus Ultra attitude?" said Mic.

"But forcing it in would surely stretch out poor Eri's sock," protested Thirteen.

"Forget the sock already," said Aizawa, but before he could scold his frantic colleagues any further, they all heard a faint noise and whipped around. They saw motion outside the window and instantly panicked. A villain, perhaps? Eri was sleeping just a few feet from the window, so when a dark figure started to open it, the four teachers leaped into fighting stances, prepared to defend the girl. The window slid open, but before the perpetrator could climb in, Aizawa's binding cloth shot out and wrapped around the intruder's neck.

"Urk!"

"Vlad?"

Vlad King—dressed up in his own Santa suit—tumbled into the room through the window, yanked by the binding cloth.

"Hey! Vlad! Huh?" came a worried voice from outside. A moment later, Hound Dog peered through the window sporting a set of fake reindeer antlers. Apparently these two had gone for a whole dual cosplay for Eri's sake. In any case, all the hubbub was disturbing enough that Eri began to stir, prompting every adult in the room to drop to the floor, which was when they noticed the gleaming white eyes and teeth lurking in the darkness under the bed itself. Every instinct told them to scream at the sight of what had to be some sort of boogeyman, but they managed to swallow down their cries for Eri's sake. Once the girl was sound asleep again, a black figure appeared before them and said "Shh" with one finger to its mouth.

"Don't scare us like that, Ectoplasm," said Midnight.

"My heart flatlined for a second there!" said Mic.

The real Ectoplasm (also wearing a Santa costume) emerged from under the bed to join his Quirk-created clone. He'd arrived in the room before any of them, but when the rest of the crew had started showing up, he'd missed his chance to make himself known and join them.

"Apologies," he said, as his clone dissipated. "I feared that calling out would frighten you all and alert Eri to our presence."

"Can I come in now?" asked Hound Dog, who'd been cowering outside the window.

A moment later, all seven teachers were huddled together near the door for another meeting.

"Lemme get this straight—we're all here to deliver gifts to Eri?" asked Mic.

Vlad King and Hound Dog nodded.

"That's right," said Vlad. "Me and Hound Dog pulled out all the stops to keep the fantasy alive for Eri."

"Down to the last detail, huh," said Midnight, flicking Hound Dog's fake antlers.

"Yep. Cementoss whipped these up for me," said Hound Dog. "And Power Loader motorized our sleigh for us—no pulling needed." Although Cementoss and Power Loader hadn't come themselves, they'd gone in on the teddy bear with Thirteen.

Like the others, Vlad King had been spending some free time with Eri, teaching her gymnastics exercises. She'd had trouble getting the hang of it at first, but these days she'd get a real thrill when Vlad King lifted her overhead and she pretended to be an airplane. She'd even taken to calling him "Mister Exercise," which had inspired him to find books on entertaining exercise routines for children.

Hound Dog, meanwhile, was still a little scary to Eri, given his role as the strict school life supervisor. Still, after he'd taught Eri which wildflowers smelled the sweetest, she'd drawn a picture of those very flowers for him—a picture he had promptly hung up in his room.

"I am here to leave CDs of nursery rhymes as a gift," said Ectoplasm.

Eri had also been scared of Ectoplasm at first, and after he'd presented for her his "clone-powered canon" rendition of a children's song in an effort to win her over, she'd gone from scared to terrified. Midnight and Thirteen had later joined Ectoplasm's performances, however, which had made the girl comfortable enough to start calling him "Mister Song." Now he'd brought a set of mix CDs loaded with handpicked songs just for Eri.

"I don't believe Eri owns a CD player, though," said Thirteen.

"She doesn't?" said Ectoplasm.

"Hey, no prob!" said Mic. "The deejaying set I'm gifting her can play CDs!"

"What'd you two get for her?" Midnight asked Vlad King and Hound Dog. "I got her a book."

"A cute comb, an adorable hairpin, and a lovely little hand mirror," said Hound Dog.

"Well, lookit you two, trying to win her over with girlie-girl stuff!" said Mic.

"I actually asked the girls in my class for advice," said Vlad King, sounding smug.

"Dang! We shoulda gone that route too!" said Mic.

"No, I am quite grateful for your choice of the dee-jaying set," said Ectoplasm.

"Speaking of presents, how about we deliver them?" said Aizawa, his low voice cutting through the chatter like a knife. He knew that if they dawdled too long, Eri might wake up and their whole surprise would be spoiled. His grave tone brought the others to their senses, helping them focus on the mission at hand. A bit more debate over the tiny-sock issue led to the decision not to try cramming any of the presents inside. After all, it wasn't the sock that mattered—it was the presents.

Once more, the group of teachers snuck over to the bed, where the sight of Eri's cherubic face and the sound of her soft breathing warmed their hearts. But as they attempted to place the presents by her pillow, the angel figurine on the shelf came to life, its eyes glowing red. Before they could react, two halves of a transparent, dome-like shield shot up from either side of the bed, meeting in the middle and sealing the bed within, Eri and all.

"What the—?"

Aizawa attempted to pry open the shield to rescue Eri, but the thin material was tougher than it looked and wouldn't budge. That was when the angel floated into the air.

"*Intruders detected. Intruders detected,*" announced the angel in a robotic voice before it began firing off weaponized beams. The teachers dodged in the nick of time, but the beams kept coming, forcing them to dance around the cramped room.

"What the heck's this about?" said Mic.

"No clue, but we've got to help dear Eri," said Midnight.

And yet Eri was still fast asleep under the clear dome, so they realized it must be soundproof.

"Wait a minute!" said Thirteen with a gasp. "At the end of the meeting today, didn't the principal say something about improved security?"

The others searched their memories, trying to recall exactly what Principal Nezu had said.

"It was, 'Ah, one more thing! Keep in mind that as of today, we've bolstered security measures...in Eri's room'!" screamed Mic.

Power Loader had modeled the Guardian Angelbot after one of Hatsume's toy monkeys, but at the moment, he was in the underground dungeon tinkering away, none the wiser that his defense system had been installed earlier.

"Whoa!"

"Yikes!"

The flurry of beams somehow corralled them all into one corner, at which point the Angelbot spoke again.

"Capture intruders. Capture intruders."

A powerful, sticky rope launched from the angel and wrapped around the teachers. Following its programming, the machine had determined that, based on the size of the room and the number of "villains," the optimal strategy was to herd them into a group with the beams before binding them with the rope.

"Oh, great…" said Mic.

"Grr! Can't get this sticky crap offa me!" said Hound Dog.

"How're we ever gonna deliver our presents now?" moaned Midnight.

In response, Ectoplasm created one of his clones, and Thirteen aimed one of her fingers at the Angelbot, ready to produce a black hole with her Quirk.

"Shall I destroy it?" said Ectoplasm.

"Should I suck it up?" said Thirteen.

"Probably shouldn't, when the principal went outta his way to install it," said Vlad King, voicing his disapproval for the plan.

"What's our move, then?" asked Mic.

"We'll have to disable it without destroying it," said Aizawa, after a moment of thought. "Then we drop the presents and leave." He eyed the Guardian Angelbot— still floating overhead and monitoring the group— before explaining the plan in a whisper.

"Ectoplasm—you distract the machine while Thirteen destroys the rope. Once we're free, Vlad and I will

pin down that angel. In the meantime, the rest of you will…"

"Leave the presents?" said Midnight.

"Okay! We can handle that part!" said Mic.

"After that, maybe we should split into two teams for the escape?" suggested Midnight.

"I will open the door," said Ectoplasm, "and Hound Dog can open the window. When the operation is finished, each of you leave via the nearest exit."

The teachers nodded in agreement and glanced over at Eri, who was still sleeping peacefully. The notion of safeguarding the girl's innocent dreams brought a deadly serious look to their faces as their pride as pro heroes kicked in.

"The first move is yours, Ectoplasm," said Aizawa.

Ectoplasm unleashed about fifteen clones all at once to surround the Angelbot, and Thirteen wriggled around for a moment before popping open one of her space suit's fingertips.

"Here I go!" said Thirteen, but the bindings and awkward angle made her finger slip, causing the ensuing black hole to suck in every last one of Ectoplasm's clones, which shrieked in agony as they were swallowed up. The loss of the clones had no physical effect on the original Ectoplasm, but the shock filled him with a vicarious fear of gruesome death.

"Their lives flashed before my eyes!" he cried at Thirteen.

"S-so sorry! My attack is hard to aim with a high degree of accuracy. Here, let me try again…"

Thirteen's black holes were like kisses of instant death, and her colleagues were suddenly keenly aware that another deadly orb was about to be unleashed in their immediate vicinity.

"Careful with those things!" yelped Mic. "Maybe try aiming from this direction?"

"Ah, please don't jostle me so much," said Thirteen, but Mic's panicked fidgeting resulted in another misfire—one that sucked up Hound Dog's reindeer antlers.

"Awooo…" came his mournful howl as his face went pale.

"Aim right this time!" said Vlad King. "It'd put the school in a real bind if we all got sucked up and somehow Mic was the only one left!"

"O-okay!" said Thirteen.

"Ouch, Vlad! And quit putting pressure on Thirteen," said Mic.

"Please do it quickly! Ah!" said Ectoplasm. The Angelbot had evaded his next wave of clones and was once again staring down at the teachers. Its smile—which might have appeared kind and merciful in better times—took on a haughty, sneering quality in the dark and gloom, as if the angel were presiding over inferior creatures. Less like an angel of heaven, more like a demon of hell.

Aizawa and the teachers gulped, realizing that they had a long and miserable night ahead of them. Eri, meanwhile, was still fast asleep, blissfully unaware that outside her bubble, this holy night had turned into desperate struggle for survival.

UA

The creeping morning light hit Eri's still-closed eyes. Reluctant to leave dreamland just yet, she spun around in bed and managed to hit something with her flailing arm.

"Hmm? Oh!"

At the sight of the pile of presents covering her pillow and then some, Eri's eyes sparkled as bright as the morning sun. In an instant she was fully awake, eager to confirm that she wasn't dreaming. Yes, the gifts were real. Clad in her pajamas, she dashed out of her room and down the hall and found Aizawa on the sofa in the communal area.

"G-good morning," said Eri.

"Oh? Morning," said Aizawa.

"Um, last night, I think Santa came and... Wait, huh?"

Splayed out on the couch were Present Mic, Midnight, Thirteen, Ectoplasm, Vlad King, and Hound Dog. They'd spent most of the night locked in a death battle with the Guardian Angelbot and had only managed to claim victory and clean up the room less than an hour before. Unable to muster the strength to return to their own beds, they'd flopped down on the sofa in the aftermath. Aizawa himself had slept like a log briefly, and it was taking all he had to sit upright at the moment.

"Good morning, Eri..." said Midnight.

"Ah, good morning," said Eri, always one to mind her manners. She found it odd how exhausted all the teachers were, but her excitement got the better of her.

"Um, so, I think Santa came...and brought me lots of presents."

"Oh yeah? That's great," said Aizawa.

"Uh-huh," said Eri, who was positively beaming by this point. It was a smile powerful enough to penetrate the teachers' fatigue and turn up the corners of their mouths. Having done their duty as both heroes and grown-ups, they turned to each other and exchanged the knowing glances that can only be shared by weary comrades in arms. Such was the power behind Eri's pure smile—a reward that made it all worth it, and the best Christmas present they could have asked for.

After thanking her pro hero bodyguard, Tsuyu Asui walked up to the door of her house for the first time in a good while.

Has Samidare been looking after Satsuki properly? Are they both doing their homework? Oh, right—we'll have to do the winter cleaning before Mom and Dad get home. Mom said she's picking up the osechi *food for New Year's and that we already have soba noodles in the house...*

It was out of old habit that Tsuyu went over this laundry list of tasks to handle. Her parents' work sent them both on frequent business trips, so before the dorm system had been implemented, Tsuyu had been largely responsible for minding her brother Samidare—the middle sibling—and her sister Satsuki—the youngest. In this moment, she knew that cataloging the tasks in her head would let her leap into action more efficiently once inside, and any free time that remained would be set aside for studying.

As she reached for the doorknob, Tsuyu suddenly felt transported back to her pre-U.A. days, and she let out a few ribbity chuckles in spite of herself.

"Welcome home, Tsuyu."

"Yeah, welcome."

Waiting for her in the entryway were Samidare and Satsuki, both wearing aprons.

"Hi, you two. Did you get hungry and start making dinner early?" asked Tsuyu.

"Naw, this is because I'm on bathroom cleaning duty," said Samidare.

"I'm cleaning the kitchen," said Satsuki. Both siblings defiantly placed their hands akimbo.

Tsuyu was shocked. They'd helped her wash dishes in the past, but they'd never really engaged in full-blown housecleaning.

"Mom and Dad did the big cleaning last Sunday, and we've already got water boiling for the soba, so you should take a load off in your room, Tsuyu," said Samidare.

"We got tea and snacks ready for you too," said Satsuki.

"But…"

"No *buts* allowed," said Samidare, as he and Satsuki shoved their reluctant big sister down the hall and into her old room. Tsuyu peeked through the door and observed that her siblings had legitimately been cleaning.

"Ribbit…"

She'd been prepared to tackle all sorts of chores upon arriving home, so this almost felt anticlimactic. Mulling this over, Tsuyu discovered freshly brewed tea and some snacks on the table, just as promised.

They're really growing up, aren't they?

Internalizing this fact suddenly made her miss them dearly. Naturally, she'd worried about how her siblings would fare when she'd had to leave home, so learning that they could actually fend for themselves to this extent conjured a mixture of melancholy and joy.

"Well, who am I to reject this hospitality?" said Tsuyu to herself.

As she finally started to relax with the tea and snacks, her phone rang. It was her old friend Habuko Mongoose.

"Hello? Habuko?"

"Tsuyu! How's it hanging? Didja get home yet? I feel like it's been forever!"

"Wait, how did you know I'm visiting home?"

"Your little bro filled me in!"

Time flew by as Tsuyu and Habuko recounted the latest goings-on in their lives. They chatted about school, friends, and their recent obsessions, and it felt like the conversation might never end…if not for a loud crash from the Asui family kitchen.

"Sorry, Habuko, I'll call you back," said Tsuyu, dashing out of her room toward the kitchen.

She arrived to find a cooking pot lying on the floor, surrounded by water that had clearly been inside the pot until a moment ago. Nearby, her brother and sister stood stupefied.

"What happened?"

"I dropped the pot…" said Samidare.

"It was heavier than he thought," added Satsuki.

"You were trying to make soba, right? That's okay, let me take over."

As Tsuyu reached for the fallen pot, she saw her siblings slump gloomily and noticed a bandage on one of Samidare's fingertips. It instantly reminded her of the days she had spent learning to cook, way back when.

They've really been trying.

Tsuyu stood and gave them both pats on the head.

"Actually, why don't we make the soba together?" suggested Tsuyu. "Is that okay with you two?"

Samidare and Satsuki stared at Tsuyu's warm smile, and then at each other. After a moment of silent consultation, they gave a cheery "Okay!" in unison. Tsuyu texted Habuko to let her know what had happened and promised to chat again another time. Now they needed time to get down to business.

The three Asui siblings set the pot over the stove, prepared the dipping sauce, chopped the chives, set up the colander, and laid out the plates and bowls. Watching her brother and sister take the lead, Tsuyu suddenly recalled her kakizome homework assignment concerning an aspiration for the coming year.

How about 和 (wa)? As in "peace and harmony," since that's all I want for my brother and sister when I can't be here for them.

This thought brought a smile to Tsuyu's face, just as she heard her parents calling out "We're home!" from the entryway.

"Welcome home," croaked all three kids.

With the whole family united again, more smiles were sure to follow.

Part 3
Awkward Year's-End Soba

IF THERE'S ANYTHING YOU CAN'T EAT, DON'T WORRY.

"**W**elcome home, Shoto!"

Shoto Todoroki had barely taken his shoes off in the entryway when he heard his older sister shout from deeper in the house, followed by the pitter-patter of her slippered shoes rushing toward him. Wiping her wet hands on her apron, Fuyumi gave her little brother a broad, warm smile.

"Thanks," said Shoto.

It was New Year's Eve, and the students had been given permission to visit home for that night and the following day, as long as they had a pro hero escorting them.

"I was so sure you wouldn't be home for the holiday, so this was a pleasant surprise. You hungry?" said Fuyumi.

"No… Are you making something?" said Shoto, walking toward the kitchen. A bevy of tantalizing aromas filled his nose.

"Yes, just the traditional osechi stuff," said Fuyumi. "Ah, the water's boiling!"

Shoto watched as his sister ran over, lowered the fire, and breathed a sigh of relief. The main work space was already covered with cooked dishes, including *kuromame* (sweet black soybeans), *tazukuri* (candied sardines), *kurikinton* (candied chestnuts and sweet potatoes), and *datemaki* (sweet rolled omelet). The sight of it all reminded him that this lavish spread was just another yearly tradition.

Shoto's hand instinctively reached out for the glossy black kuromame, but Fuyumi caught him and said, "Nuh-uh! Not until you wash your hands, mister."

"Fine," he said, marching off to the bathroom.

"So are you hungry or not? I can make you something else," called Fuyumi, still in the kitchen.

"No," said Shoto. "I already ate with Mom."

He'd gotten permission to add an extra stop to his homecoming so he could visit his mother, Rei, in the institution where she was kept. Those visits had become

rarer since the dorm system had been implemented, so Shoto hadn't been about to let this valuable opportunity pass him by. As it happened, Rei was doing well enough that her doctors implied she might be discharged in the near future. As Shoto washed his hands and gargled for a bit, he recalled the meal he and his mother had just shared in the hospital cafeteria.

Her gentle face rose up in his mind. As he recalled their rambling conversation about nothing in particular, it occurred to him that this had been the first meal they'd eaten together in years. He remembered how the cafeteria had been all out of soba (the not-hot kind), so Rei had chosen beef stew instead, and Shoto had opted for *katsudon*. Beef stew and katsudon—the favorite foods and frequent orders of two of his good friends. He remembered telling his mother how finishing the supplemental course meant that he'd earned his provisional hero license. Finally, he remembered her parting words to him: "I'm making an effort too."

"I know, Mom. I'll try even harder," mumbled Shoto, staring into the bathroom mirror. His own efforts concerned his dream to become an all-powerful hero, like the one he'd seen on TV as a little boy. It was only recently that he realized he'd been taking the long way around toward his dream for years out of sheer hatred for his father, who'd abused his mother. Going forward, his path was straight ahead, no detours.

Shoto walked back into the kitchen and popped a kuromame bean into his mouth. Fuyumi noticed and rolled her eyes affectionately.

"Is it good, at least?" she asked. Shoto nodded.

"Glad to hear it. Ah, Natsu's also coming home today… Dad too," said Fuyumi.

"Hrm."

Fuyumi wore a troubled smile in response to her brother's cryptic grunt, which couldn't exactly be read as positive or negative. Shoto suddenly felt bad for his sister.

"Can I help?" he said.

"Nonsense. You're only home once in a blue moon, so take it easy," said Fuyumi.

Shoto looked unsure how to respond, so his sister smiled at him.

"Fine, fine. Your futon's drying by the window in your room. Why don't you take it down and lay it out?"

"Okay."

|A|

"I'm home!" said Natsuo, stepping into the entryway. He immediately spotted a pair of unfamiliar shoes— loafers, characteristic of schoolkids.

Ah. Must be Shoto's.

Fuyumi had told him that their little brother would be home tonight. The shoes in question were scuffed and a bit dirty, but otherwise pretty ordinary. Natsuo stared at them for a moment.

"Hi, Natsu! Hey, what's the holdup out there?"

The sound of his sister scampering toward him snapped Natsuo out of his reverie, and he took off his own shoes and stepped into the hall.

"Nothing," he said. "I take it Shoto's here already?"

"Mm-hm. Actually, I wonder what's keeping him?" said Fuyumi.

"Keeping him? What's he up to?"

"I told him to lay out his futon, but that was a while ago," said Fuyumi, glancing in the general direction of Shoto's room.

"Lemme go check on him," said Natsuo.

"Thanks. Hang on—weren't you going to bring home the girlfriend?" teased Fuyumi. She peered over his shoulder mockingly, as if he might be hiding someone behind him.

"Ugh!" he grunted with a scowl, clearly embarrassed. "She's spending the holiday with her fam too... but we're gonna do *hatsumode* together at some point. First shrine visit of the New Year and all."

Now it was Fuyumi's turn to cringe with an "Ugh!" of her own.

"You're so darn *innocent* it makes me sick!" she said.

"Oh, gimme a break! You asked!" said Natsuo.

"That's enough out of you. Go wash your hands," said Fuyumi.

"Fine. Whatever you say," he said, marching off to the bathroom.

"Oh, also..." said Fuyumi. She paused, preparing to adorn her words with a practiced air of nonchalance.

"Dad's coming home early today, after work. And he said he's bringing home a feast."

"Yeah? Then I'll make sure to be long gone before he gets here."

"Natsu..."

His sister had expected that reaction, but still her face clouded over. Though it hurt Natsuo's heart to see his sister so dejected, he was in no mood to change his mind.

"Sorry, but..." he started.

"Anyhow, you'll have some year's-end soba, right? Homemade, of course," interrupted Fuyumi, who, hoping to break the awkward tension, grinned and rolled up her sleeves. Unable to resist her jovial efforts, Natsuo sighed and decided to play along.

"Sis, don't tell me you're gonna quit teaching to become a noodle-monger!"

"I dunno! Maybe! The local soba master said I've got the knack for it."

After the lighthearted back-and-forth, Natsuo washed his hands, as promised, and moved toward the side room. As he opened the sliding shoji panel and stepped in, he caught a whiff of incense. This particular room held the butsudan altar for family members who'd passed away, and it always felt like a space where time had stopped. Perhaps that was because, for Natsuo, his brother Toya would forever remain the age he was in the photo on the altar.

"Hmm?"

Natsuo was about to light an incense stick when he noticed the dying embers of another, already in the incense burner.

Was Shoto in here earlier?

Natsuo's brow furrowed, and he was suddenly overcome with emotion at the thought of his little brother offering incense at the altar. There was nothing strange about the act—they were family, after all—but Natsuo instinctively bristled at the very notion of being a part of *this* family, which was hardly an ordinary one.

"I'm home, Toya..."

After placing a lit stick of incense, Natsuo got up and moved toward Shoto's room, which he rarely had occasion to visit.

"Shoto?" he said, facing the sliding fusuma screen.

No response. Natsuo slid the screen aside, not expecting to find his brother inside, but there he was—fast asleep on the futon that he'd clearly plopped down onto without much care, all askew. Moving quietly so as not to wake Shoto, Natsuo crept over and peered at his brother's face. He looked surprisingly young, despite the burn scar that sat heavy on his face like a shadow. Having been abused by Endeavor—who'd been fixated

on his own ambition—Rei Todoroki had snapped one day and thrown scalding water in Shoto's face. Natsuo would never forget the pair of tear-filled screams he'd heard that day. *How painful it must have been*, he thought.

Natsuo caught himself extending a finger toward the scar but quickly curled it away when he realized what he was doing. Shoto's scar probably wouldn't exist if only the boy hadn't inherited aspects of both his parents' Quirks. Maybe Shoto could have enjoyed a normal childhood, full of carefree days playing with his siblings.

And yet I couldn't do a thing...

Natsuo had been in elementary school when it had happened. Their father, Endeavor, had ignored his family's well-being in pursuit of his ambitions—ambitions he'd projected onto young Shoto. Even now, Natsuo would beat himself up over how he used to be before the abuse really began, recalling the period in his life that had made him feel pathetic and ashamed. Before Shoto was born, Natsuo had sought his father's love and care, and when Endeavor was around, he would turn into an excited ball of energy, eager for attention.

But that love never came. It was only thanks to his warm and caring mother that Natsuo had survived those early years and learned to cope with rejection from his other parent. But after Shoto was born, even their mother grew distant, though not out of indifference. Natsuo could sense how much energy she'd had to devote to protecting her youngest, her baby, from her husband's so-called training—which most would label abuse—but at that age, Natsuo couldn't help but feel that his mother had been stolen away from him. After witnessing his mother and brother crying and screaming on that horrible day, Natsuo had been overcome with crushing shame.

He found himself unable to stare at his brother's childlike face any longer, so he left the room and moved to the kitchen.

"Did you say hi to Shoto?" asked Fuyumi.

"He's asleep," said Natsuo.

"Poor thing must be exhausted," said Fuyumi with a soft smile, picturing her little brother. "Oh, can you grab the *jubako* for me?"

Natsuo fetched the stacked serving boxes from the cabinet and started working on other kitchen tasks.

"Why'd we have to be born as Endeavor's children, huh?" he mumbled, unable to hold it in anymore.

"Huh? Please, no heavy topics. Not right now," said Fuyumi. She produced another smile as she continued her work, though it was a slightly troubled one.

"I'm just saying," said Natsuo. "Imagine how we could've been, as an actually happy family."

"Natsu, please..."

"I know, I know, even normal families've got problems, but...it only turned out this way cuz he married Mom for her Quirk. So how dare he go and..."

Natsuo felt the rage welling up and cut himself off. He was eager to vent, but the one he really wanted to take his anger out on wasn't there. Not that their father would even fight back, at this point.

"Nah, forget it!" said Natsuo, swallowing his anger and frustration while forcing a fake smile.

"Talking about *him* just pisses me off," he continued, "and now I'm hungry!"

He popped one of the datemaki omelet bites in his mouth.

"Mm-mmm! No one makes datemaki quite like you, Sis."

Fuyumi's troubled expression softened into a relieved smile.

"That's Mom's recipe, of course," she said. "But no snacking! Load those into the jubako, won't you?"

"Okaaay... Should I stick them in this part?"

"Yes, right there," said Fuyumi. "Like other rolled foods, datemaki usually represent good luck with studies and schoolwork, but Mom's parents taught her to make this rounder version, which is a way of wishing for a harmonious household—like everyone coming together in a big circle. That's why I put so much love and energy into these every year."

As she spoke, Fuyumi violated her own rule and ate the end slice of datemaki.

"Delicious, as expected," she said with a self-satisfied nod, before noticing that Natsuo seemed at a loss for words.

"What is it?" she asked.

The nonchalant question caught Natsuo off guard. He realized his hands had stopped moving, so he resumed his task and placed the rest of the soft datemaki into the box gently, careful to keep it from falling apart.

"It's nothing," he said.

"Really?"

"Yeah, really. You don't gotta treat me like a kid."

Natsuo nearly gasped at his words, which sounded wholly unconvincing even to his ear. He had been a kid, back then. And Shoto had been even younger.

"Sis, I... Sometimes...sometimes I wish I'd done more to stop him when he was being such a monster to Shoto..."

Fuyumi spun around to look at her brother, who furrowed his brow and tried to keep the mood from getting any darker with a "Wait, just hear me out."

"Shoto was so little back then," he continued. "It's not like he could run away or anything, no matter how bad he wanted to. Sure, Endeavor barely even acknowledged our existence, which wasn't great, but it was kinda no big deal compared to the crap he did to Shoto."

When he was finished, his sister set down the long cooking chopsticks and gave him a gentle pat on the head. Natsuo looked confused.

"I know you suffered in your own way, and that's perfectly valid," she said. "You don't have to compare your pain to anyone else's."

Fuyumi's warm and earnest gaze made Natsuo shut his eyes tight and bite his lower lip. These two had been in it together since the start, so he was terrible at hiding anything from her. Yes, he'd endured his own pain, but the feeling that he'd failed in his role as Shoto's big brother still haunted him.

"Natsu?"

Natsuo turned to find his little brother standing at the entrance to the kitchen, still looking half-asleep. Based on the confused look on his face, it appeared Shoto had witnessed Fuyumi patting Natsuo's head.

"Oh, you're up," said Natsuo. "I found you snoozing a minute ago. Isn't that right, *Sis*?"

Eager to move on and not have Shoto ask questions, Natsuo punctuated his words and gave his sister a sharp glance.

"Yes, you were sleeping so peacefully that Natsu didn't want to disturb you," said Fuyumi.

"Oh, I had no idea," said Shoto with a small yawn. "You could've woken me up."

Natsuo gave an imperceptible sigh of relief, glad that Shoto hadn't overheard anything.

"Let me help," said the youngest Todoroki, stepping into the kitchen, but Fuyumi had ideas of her own.

"Leave the kitchen to me," she said. "Why don't you two go outside and feed the koi instead?"

A

At first, her brothers insisted that feeding the fish wasn't a task that took two people, but Fuyumi insisted and forced them out into the garden.

Oh, you're good, Sis...

Natsuo scowled a little, knowing full well that Fuyumi's ulterior motive was to try to force her younger brothers to bond. Silently, Shoto followed behind him. They'd spoken face-to-face few enough times in their lives to count on two hands, and Natsuo had only recently learned that Shoto's favorite food was soba. Despite living in the same household, he felt so guilty about their childhood that he'd actually spent much more time in the room of his dead brother than in that of his living one. In fact, Natsuo still wasn't quite comfortable being alone with Shoto, given how infrequent their interactions were. Acting normal seemed impossible when their relationship was anything but.

Makes sense, though, in a family that's not normal at all.

This thought seemed to drain Natsuo and forced his mouth into a weary half smile.

"Natsu?"

At Shoto's questioning tone, Natsuo turned to find a puzzled look on his brother's face. Those two-tone eyes had once held a darkness within them and had emitted a smoldering energy that seemed to reject everyone and everything. At some recent point, however, Shoto had undergone a dramatic change.

"Shoto's already made friends at U.A."

That's what his overjoyed mother had told Natsuo when he'd visited. Maybe it was those friends who had brought about this change? Suddenly, he felt the urge to meet these friends of Shoto's.

"Erm, it's nothing," said Natsuo, at last. He had been about to ask about his brother's friends but suddenly felt awkward.

When they arrived at the pond, the koi started swarming at the edge by the boys' feet, their gaping mouths at the ready.

"They must be hungry," said Shoto quietly.

The brothers walked to the storage shed and started rummaging around for the fish food. The large shed was packed with gardening tools and abandoned relics of years gone by.

"Now where's that food?" said Natsuo. "Wait, hmm?" He'd encountered something near the fish food that gave him a twinge of nostalgia—their old soccer ball. It showed signs of age but was still inflated enough to be used.

Right. This old thing...

Holding the ball, Natsuo whipped around and called out to his brother, who was inspecting the unfamiliar space as if it were a lost tomb.

"Think fast!"

He'd thrown the ball hoping to surprise his brother, fully expecting that Shoto's U.A.-honed reflexes would kick in and help him catch it, but instead Shoto's eyes bulged wide in surprise and the ball bounced off his body. Natsuo didn't know how to react to this awkward development and stood frozen in place as Shoto ran off to retrieve the ball. The chase led him near the pond, and then...

"Watch out!" cried Natsuo as he watched his little brother stumble and fall sideways, right into the koi pond.

"Pwah!" gasped Shoto, standing up in the shallow water. He surveyed his own soaking wet body and was dismayed by how pathetic he felt. Meanwhile, Natsuo burst out laughing.

"Natsu..." said Shoto with a dark scowl.

"Sorry! C'mon, lemme help," said Natsuo, extending a hand. Shoto took it, but as he shifted his weight to clamber out of the pond, his foot slipped on the moss-covered rocks.

"Whoa!"

UA

"You *both* fell in? How does that even happen? Bath! Now!"

One look at her dripping wet brothers and Fuyumi ran off to heat the bathwater, grumbling about what a shame it would be if they caught colds during the holiday. The boys obeyed, warming their chilly bodies

with a quick shower rinse before settling into the large family-style tub, which could easily fit five.

"Ahh..." sighed Natsuo instinctively, submitting to the hot water and its soothing power. "Can't believe I took a dunk in the fishpond on New Year's Eve..."

"Sorry..." said Shoto.

"You're sorry? I'm the one who threw that ball. It was my bad."

"No... I just mean..." started Shoto. Hiss loss for words revived that same awkward discomfort in Natsuo.

C'mon. You're allowed to tell me it was my fault.

Unsure what to do with himself, Natsuo dipped his face under the water. That was when he realized this was the first time he'd ever bathed with his little brother. When he was little, he'd taken baths with his mother and older siblings, but once his mother had started bathing with Shoto, he and the others had been on their own.

"We've never taken a bath together before now," muttered Shoto.

"True enough," said Natsuo, slightly shocked that his brother had been thinking the same thing.

"How're the baths in your dorm building? Nice and big?" he continued.

"Twice as big as this one."

"I bet it's loads of fun, piling on in there with your friends."

"It's...normal. I'm used to it by now. Anyway, we should probably wash our hair, right?" said Shoto.

Natsuo agreed and suggested that Shoto go first; it was already evening, and neither of the brothers felt like bathing again later. Shoto climbed out of the tub, set a stool down by the sitting-style shower, and began to wash his hair. Natsuo watched his brother's back and spaced out. The defined muscles he saw there spoke to the training Shoto had undergone at U.A.

He's giving it his all at school, huh?

Natsuo couldn't help but be impressed by his little brother—a future pro hero. Despite the hard times they'd endured at the hands of the Todoroki family's current pro hero, Shoto was aiming for the same career. It had actually been Fuyumi who'd encouraged her little brother, which had led him to U.A. in pursuit of his dream. He wanted nothing more than to provide support for other wounded souls like his mother.

Natsuo could tell that Shoto had begun to move forward toward that dream, and he knew how much courage that took. Starting took courage, keeping it up took conviction, and Shoto was clearly lacking neither. As the big brother, Natsuo suddenly found himself feeling pathetic again, but at the same time, he was deeply proud. This blend of emotions somehow began to melt away that bristling he'd felt in his heart earlier.

"Shoto, you having fun at school?" asked Natsuo, just as his little brother was rinsing out the shampoo.

"Huh? You say something?" said Shoto, whipping around.

"I asked if school is fun."

The simple question was of no great importance, but Natsuo felt like making conversation.

"I wouldn't say 'fun,'" said Shoto. "The training is tough, and we barely have time to breathe between classes."

"Sure. Makes sense," said Natsuo.

"Not that that's a bad thing," said Shoto, looking almost pleased. Natsuo grinned.

"Y'don't say!"

"What about you? How's college?"

"It's brutal! But I'm still having a blast!"

"Sis told me you have a girlfriend."

"She never has learned to mind her own business," said Natsuo, who lowered his face into the water at the mention of the awkward topic. This earned a small smile from Shoto, and in turn, a submerged smile from Natsuo. Shoto had now begun to wash his body.

"And you? Any ladies in your life these days?" asked Natsuo, bringing his mouth back above the water line.

"No."

"No wonder, given how busy they keep you at that school. How about friends, then? Got any of those?"

Shoto hands stopped moving as he thought, but before Natsuo could say "It ain't a trick question!" Shoto gave his answer.

"Midoriya and Ida, I guess. I usually eat lunch with them, and we study together sometimes."

"Cool, cool," said Natsuo.

"I thought I might get closer with Bakugo since we had to do that license course together, but it didn't turn out that way," added Shoto.

"Hmm?" Natsuo tilted his head questioningly.

What, did they get in a fight or something?

Shoto didn't elaborate on Bakugo, but he did go down the list, mentioning each of his classmates in one way or another. As Natsuo climbed out of the bath to switch places with his brother, he felt glad he'd started this conversation.

"But seriously, what're they teaching you at that school if you can't even catch a ball?" he asked teasingly.

Shoto froze for a moment, almost embarrassed.

"It took me by surprise," he said. "That's the ball you all used to play with, years ago. I watched you, you know. Always wanted to play too."

This small confession was like a knife to Natsuo's heart, and he let the shower water hide the tears that began to form in his eyes. Stopping the abuse might've been a tall order for a child, but he could've started by inviting his little brother to play with them, if nothing else.

Natsuo furiously rinsed the shampoo out of his hair before whipping around with a smile.

"Let's play some soccer after the bath, huh?" he said.

"When we've just gotten clean?" said Shoto.

"Whatever! If we get sweaty, the bath's not going anywhere."

Before Shoto could respond, they heard the door to the changing room slide open, and Fuyumi's silhouette appeared on the other side of the fogged-up glass.

"Natsu! Shoto! I have to run out for a bit!" she said.

"Huh? For what?!" said Natsuo.

"I forgot to pick up the mochi I ordered!"

After watching their sister's scurrying ankles carry her away, the boys decided it was time to get out of the bath. They put on some clothes and moved into the kitchen, where they found the entire osechi spread waiting for them. The water in the large pot was steaming, as if the burner had been lit until just a moment ago, and a smaller pot contained fragrant soba dipping sauce. Laid out on the table were a large kneading bowl, a bag of buckwheat flour, and a rolling pin.

"Soba-making gear, huh?" remarked Natsuo. Shoto's eyes were glued to the tools and ingredients, but his expression was inscrutable. Still, in a moment of insight, Natsuo took the hint.

"Let's save the soccer for another time, yeah?" he said.

"Huh?"

"You're clearly dying to make some soba."

Shoto nodded shyly.

"I get it. You love soba," said Natsuo with a grin. "Hey—how about we pound this out before Sis gets back? That'll knock her socks off."

"Okay…"

The two brothers rolled up their sleeves and approached the flour as if ready for battle, but then Shoto froze in place.

"You, uh, wanna get started, buddy?" said Natsuo, who'd been planning to assist while Shoto did the honors.

"I do, but this is my first time. What about you, Natsu?" said Shoto.

"Same here! You think us first timers are up to the task? Hang on, lemme look it up," said Natsuo, whipping out his phone. The internet informed him that, yes, beginners might have a tough time of it.

"Doing it with nothing but buckwheat flour is hard, they say. Let's try the *nihachi* hybrid version, with a little wheat flour added in," said Natsuo.

"No. Full buckwheat," said Shoto.

"That's the hard way, though…" said Natsuo.

"I think it's tastier," insisted Shoto.

Sensing that Shoto was willing to die on this particular hill, Natsuo relented. In preparation, he looked up a simple video demonstrating the process.

"Okay… Looks like adding the water is the key step," said Natsuo. "Here we go. When the water hits, you gotta make sure it gets distributed nice and quick."

"Got it… Oops," said Shoto.

"Too much power! The flour's s'posed to stay *inside* the bowl!"

"Just add some more."

"Like this…? Aw, crap! Forgot to measure!"

"Oops again."

"I'm baaack! Sorry that took so long," said Fuyumi, who'd returned with the mochi. "Wait, what's going on here?"

Her brothers stood in the kitchen, seemingly frozen in place.

"Sorry, Sis…" said Natsuo

"We failed at soba making…" explained Shoto.

Fuyumi's eyes shifted to the table, where a *zaru* draining basket was holding an unidentifiable lump. It was the right color for soba, but its shape didn't resemble noodles in any way.

"Did you two…try making it all on your own?" she asked.

Her brothers nodded, glancing at the empty bag of flour.

"Ha ha ha!"

Fuyumi could imagine how the scene had played out, and she was almost impressed. Her brothers—who'd been bracing for a scolding—raised their eyebrows, making them look like abandoned puppy dogs.

"I got the amounts all wrong," confessed Natsuo.

"And I couldn't figure out how to mix the water in right…" said a gloomy Shoto.

"It's fine, boys. No point crying over spilled milk, right? Or flour, in this case? We'll just have to eat *that*," said Fuyumi.

"Huh?! Eat the clod?" said Natsuo.

"It's still got that soba essence, right?" said Fuyumi. "Just think of it as a dumpling rather than noodles."

"But year's-end soba is s'posed to, like…stretch across to the New Year! That's the whole point! Our lump's never gonna bridge that gap!" said Natsuo.

"Well, there's no more flour, so we'll have to deal with it," said Fuyumi.

"My soba…" mumbled Shoto, sounding mournful. His brother and sister glanced at each other, then back at him, and chuckled.

"You seriously love soba, huh," said Natsuo.

"Doesn't he, though?" added Fuyumi.

"Leave me alone," said the youngest Todoroki with a scowl, not seeing what was so funny about all this. After a moment, though, his siblings' upbeat attitude in the face of tragedy forced a smile onto even his face.

Ш

The three siblings sat down to dinner in the Japanese-style sitting room, ready to chow down on the soba clod, tempura, sashimi, and a few other dishes.

"Dad…sure is late," said Fuyumi. Endeavor would normally be home by that time, so it struck her as odd.

"Busy with work, probably," said Natsuo curtly. "Let's eat so I can get the heck out of here before he bothers showing up."

Fuyumi started to give her brother an exasperated look, but she changed her tune when she heard Natsuo's and Shoto's tummies rumbling.

"Fine. I suppose it is dinnertime," she said.

"Let's eat!" they said in unison, picking up their chopsticks and switching the TV to some bombastic year's-end programming.

"Mm-mm!" moaned Natsuo with a mouthful of sashimi, which happened to be his favorite.

"Uoyoshi's fresh fish can't be beat," said Fuyumi, referring to their favorite local fishmonger.

"It's top-tier for sure!" added Natsuo with a satisfied grin.

Next to him, Shoto chewed on a piece of the soba clod, not looking all too won over. His sister flashed a weak smile that seemed to say, "You poor thing."

I'll have to make some soba for him to take home, before he leaves tomorrow morning. Maybe Dad can pick up a new bag of flour.

Suddenly, the emcee on the variety show made a shocking announcement.

"This just in! A gigantic gorilla has climbed up Shizuoka Tower! It's believed to be the villain with the King Kong Quirk who escaped from jail just a few days ago! We have a live feed of these events, folks!"

The Todoroki siblings' eyes were now glued to the TV screen. The feed switched over to a camera at the base of Shizuoka Tower. An enormous gorilla-like creature clambered up the structure, roaring all the while.

"Yikes, that's not far from here," said Fuyumi. "Let's hope nobody gets hurt."

She'd spoken too soon—the camera zoomed in on the gorilla's hand, clearly showing a person in the monster's clutches.

"This is Sato, live on the scene! We now see that the villain has taken a hostage, and... Oh my... Is that Endeavor?!"

"Dad?" shouted Fuyumi.

When the camera revealed that the hostage was indeed their father, Natsuo coughed up the piece of sashimi he'd been working on.

"W-what the hell's he doing?" said Natsuo, sputtering.

"Yes, the hostage is none other than Endeavor! But why isn't he fighting back? Wait… Hang on, folks… It appears that the hero has something in his own hands?"

Endeavor appeared to be holding several paper shopping bags.

"Oh no! The villain is attempting to crush Endeavor in its grip!"

The camera zoomed in enough to show Endeavor's face, contorted in agony.

"Urgh… Guess I've got no choice!" shouted the hero. As he dropped the shopping bags, his entire body ignited with a burst of flame.

"Prominence…Burn!"

The bags began to fall toward the TV camera, and tumbling out of them came packages of meat, crab, *aramaki, kuzumochi*, and other groceries. But Endeavor's expanding sphere of fire caught up to the ingredients before they could get far, and the flash of heat turned them to ash in an instant.

"Ook-hohh!" roared the gorilla, wreathed in fire and now falling.

"Endeavor has beaten the villain with a single move! I hope you folks at home caught that, since it will likely

be the number one hero's final heroic act for this calendar year! But what's this? Why does Endeavor look so grumpy? Perhaps he's mad that crime never seems to let up, even during the holidays?"

Endeavor scanned the ground below, searching for any trace of the feast he had been bringing home, and out of everyone watching the spectacle, only the Todoroki siblings knew the real reason behind their father's discontent.

"I'm just glad he's okay," said a relieved Fuyumi.

"Can you believe that guy?" said Natsuo, with more than a hint of contempt.

Shoto, meanwhile, had taken his eyes off the TV and was once again focused on the soba clod.

"My soba..." he said, still unwilling to accept this travesty. His siblings smiled.

"Natsu, since Dad might be held up, why don't you relax and stay awhile?" suggested Fuyumi, nudging her brother to look at Shoto, who was nodding silently at her suggestion. Natsuo had mixed feelings on the matter, but after a moment of pretending to hesitate, he relented.

"Hrm, I guess I don't gotta rush off anywhere."

"Great. In that case, I think I'll have a little drink for the occasion. Someone gifted Dad some top-shelf stuff the other day," said Fuyumi.

When she returned with the bottle of sake, Natsuo poured some out for her.

"Here's to you, Sis! Thanks for always minding the house," he said.

"I just can't wait until you can join me for a drink," said Fuyumi.

"Gimme another year," said Natsuo, who was still only nineteen. "It'll be nice to kick one back with Shoto someday, too."

"Uh-huh," said Shoto.

"Ah, the soba dumpling pairs great with this," said Fuyumi.

"Hang on, Sis… Is *that* why you set out to make soba tonight?" asked Natsuo.

"Is soba…good with alcohol?" asked Shoto.

"Sure is. Ah, it'll be nice to share a drink with Mom once she comes home," said a grinning Fuyumi, who was fast on her way to tipsy after a few sips.

"I bet that'll be sooner rather than later," said Natsuo. After a pause, he added, "When that day comes,

we'll have to up our soba-making game for Mom, huh, Shoto?"

"Mm-hm," said Shoto with a small but resolute nod, which warmed his brother's and sister's hearts.

The TV was back to the glitzy extravaganza, but the Todoroki siblings were enjoying a low-key New Year's Eve together. All three hoped that moments like this would someday be nothing out of the ordinary.

Ochaco Uraraka was home for New Year's Eve, and she and her parents were busy enjoying each other's company and swapping endless stories late into the night. The most thrilling bit, for Ochaco, was that her father's construction business had been doing better lately. The smiles on her parents' faces as they relayed the good news brought her more joy than anything. Well, anything except for the upcoming mochi-pounding event—a local tradition on New Year's Day that she'd be joining this year.

"Hrahhh!" roared Ochaco.

"There ya go, Ochaco! Put yer back into it! We're whipping up the stickiest, tastiest mochi you ever laid eyes on!"

It was New Year's Day, and a gloved Ochaco was teamed up with an elderly neighbor. It was her job to flatten the mochi with a mallet—over and over—while her partner kneaded the dough between blows.

"You got it! Hrahh!"

When it came to her favorite food, Ochaco took no prisoners.

"Whoa, Ochaco's so intense!" said one of the neighborhood kids who'd come to watch with friends.

Steam rose from the finished product, which was handed off to another group of neighbors to be sliced, rounded, and paired with *kinako* powder, *anko* paste, sweet soy sauce, or shredded radish. There was nothing but good vibes in the air as the community started feasting on the mochi they'd created together.

"Mmm!"

Ochaco beamed with content as she scarfed down her portion of extra-stretchy mochi topped with kinako. The children were enjoying their mochi too, but then one of them gasped, suddenly remembering something.

"Hey, hey, Ochaco!" the child said, looking worried. "Is that Bakugo guy bullying you at school?"

"Huh?" said Ochaco. "Not a chance! Why d'you ask?"

"Cuz, I mean, we saw how nasty he was to you at the sports festival thing!"

Ochaco hadn't been sure where they'd gotten the idea that she was being bullied, but suddenly it clicked. They'd seen her painful defeat by Bakugo during the televised sports festival, so they were having a hard time imagining her living peacefully in the same dorm building with the boy who'd given her that merciless beatdown.

"Naw, that wasn't bullying," she explained. "He just gave me a proper fight, is all."

"You sure?"

"Mm-hm. It was real frustrating to lose that battle, but I'd rather eat an honest loss than have a guy go easy on me! In fact, that fight inspired me to work even harder, and Bakugo's really not all bad, even if he does need that dirty mouth washed out with soap!"

"That's good that he's not bullying you! But he should stop saying bad words, huh."

"On the other hand," mused Ochaco, "if he cleaned up his act, I dunno if Bakugo would really be Bakugo anymore, y'know?"

After conquering one helping of each mochi variety, Ochaco challenged herself to round two. As she returned with her refilled plate, her parents beckoned her to sit by them.

"There's just something different about digging into mochi you pounded, Ochaco!" said her father.

"You can thank these guns for that," boasted Ochaco, flexing her biceps.

"Oh, we can tell," said her mother, who gave one of her daughter's arms a squeeze.

"Heh heh," chuckled Ochaco, clearly tickled pink by the praise.

"But how's that winter homework coming along?" asked her father. "Not gonna leave it 'til the last second like always, right?"

"I-I'm on top of it! Getting it done, y'know. Erm, but I forgot all about the kakizome assignment," said Ochaco.

"Kakizome? What is this, kindergarten?"

"Aizawa Sensei doesn't want us losing too much focus over the break, I guess. We're s'posed to represent an aspiration for the coming year. Any ideas?"

"I'd go with 商売繁盛 (shobai hanjou), hoping for success in business," said Ochaco's father.

"I just want a safe, happy home so that sentiment 家内安全 (*kanai anzen*) gets my vote," said her mother.

"焼肉定食 (*yakiniku teishoku*) could be a good option. Everyone loves a grilled-meat combo platter," added her father.

"I'm not writing a menu, Dad!" said Ochaco with a laugh. Suddenly she found herself wondering what Izuku Midoriya would write.

What about using 努力 (douryoku) for "effort"? Or maybe something with a Plus Ultra or All Might theme?

A goofy grin spread across her face, which made her mother ask, "What's up?"

"Naw, s'nothing," insisted Uraraka, but her mother was too shrewd for that.

"We know your grades are fine," she said under her breath, "but how about the social side of things? Any crushes?"

"Huhh?" yelped Uraraka, whose face turned red in a flash.

"Ohh, I see," said her mother, grinning. Her father, on the other hand, went pale.

"O-Ochaco, say it ain't so... You don't got a special someone already, do you?"

"N-no way!" said Ochaco. "Who? Me? Naw! Nuh-uh!"

But every utterance of denial seemed to send her father deeper into shock.

"Boyfriend... Engagement... Marriage!" he said, as visions of his daughter's future flashed before his eyes, which were quickly filling with tears.

"It's too soon...for my little girl to be a blushing bride!"

"You're the one who needs to slow down, Dad!" said Ochaco.

"What's that? Sweet li'l Ochaco's getting married?" said a neighbor, who'd overheard the conversation.

"Who's the lucky feller?" said one old man. "Lemme read 'im the riot act to make sure he's worthy!"

"There's no 'lucky feller'!" said a beet red Ochaco to the gathering crowd.

"You gotta stop running your mouth, dear!" said her mother, punching her husband's arm.

"My Ochaco..." blubbered Ochaco's father, fully in the throes of his extended delusion.

Once the hubbub had subsided, Ochaco took a deep breath and got back to her beloved mochi.

"Stupid Dad…" she grumbled, but at the same time, she knew it all came from a place of love.

Marriage could very well be in her future, but she couldn't spend time thinking about that now. There was too much else to focus on if she was ever to grow into a hero who could bring smiles to the masses.

As Ochaco bit into her anko mochi, stretching it out into a long strand, it came to her.

I'll do 餅 (mochi) for my kakizome! Since mochi is tough and tenacious, just like how I wanna be!

She popped the piece of mochi into her mouth— stretchy strand and all—and the chewy, anko-covered treat filled her with satisfaction like nothing else.

It was the first day of the New Year, and Ochaco was feeling energized and inspired.

Part 4
New Year's with a Childhood Friend

A few days had gone by since Izuku Midoriya, Katsuki Bakugo, and Shoto Todoroki had started their new work study at Endeavor's agency.

The robber grunted as he dashed into a labyrinth of alleyways, and as he did, a huge volume of smoke billowed from his body, courtesy of his Quirk. The three would-be heroes—in hot pursuit—could no longer see their target, but they dove into the maze nonetheless.

"Kacchan! Todoroki! You two circle around, and we'll hit him from three sides!" said Midoriya, covering his mouth with his arm.

"Don't order me around!" snapped Bakugo.

"Got it," said Todoroki.

Despite Bakugo's explosive protest, he dashed down a side alley without a moment's hesitation, while Todoroki used his ice to speed along the opposite path. Midoriya sensed that his partners had changed tactics, so he kept moving forward, relying on the density of the smoke to deduce the villain's route. The three boys had already memorized the layout of this district, so they weren't totally in the dark—or the smoke, as it were.

If this goes as planned, we'll catch the villain right where the paths meet back up!

Midoriya picked up speed as he plunged through the smoke, but just as the villain came into view at the rendezvous point, a scorching whip-shaped plume of fire shot down from above and lassoed the man.

"Too slow. If you're already wiped out, then take a break," spat Endeavor, who emerged from up ahead just as the villain lost the will to fight back and the smoke cleared. Despite the win, there was no hint of mirth on the hero's face.

Endeavor might have risen to the spot of number one hero only because of All Might's impromptu retirement, but his skills were the genuine article. Within his set jurisdiction, he tackled all three fundamentals of

heroism—rescue, evacuation, and battle—on his own, so it was hard to claim that the number one hero title had gone to the wrong guy.

"I ain't wiped out!" screamed Bakugo in clear frustration.

But the boys had every right to be exhausted, after days upon days of long patrols and an early start that particular morning. And yet Endeavor showed no sign of slowing down, despite putting in even longer hours. It wasn't a fair comparison to begin with—the current number one versus students with only their provisional licenses. Nevertheless, Bakugo wouldn't make excuses for himself as he shot for the stars.

Endeavor has the home-turf advantage, of course, but we were right on that villain's tail... Ah, I get it now. He lured the villain into the alley in hopes of preventing property damage, then swung ahead to make the capture... Pro heroes never fail to impress!

As Midoriya ran through his on-site analysis of Endeavor's actions in his head, Todoroki hissed "Dammit!" under his breath. More than just pure frustration, the look in his eyes suggested a determination to observe his father's every move for his own improvement.

During this winter work study, the trio had been tasked with beating Endeavor to the punch just once. Every villain so far had been brought down by the fiery hero, however, and it was all the boys could do to keep up with his pace.

After handing over the smoke villain to the Flaming Sidekickers, Endeavor's phone rang.

"What is it? Mm-hm. Got it," was his side of the brief conversation.

"Change of plans. Deku and Bakugo—you two take a breather. Shoto—you're with me," said Endeavor.

"Why *just* me?" asked Todoroki.

"Gotta do an interview. Should be over quick enough. This is part of the job too, y'know."

"Fine."

There was no fighting Endeavor's orders, so Todoroki said "See you later" to the other two and went off with his father. Their relationship wasn't good by any stretch of the imagination, but it seemed that some of the fire had died down during the course of this work study.

Before resuming patrol, one of the Flaming Sidekickers suggested that Midoriya and Bakugo get lunch somewhere.

"Where should we go to eat?" said Midoriya.

"Like I care! Find your own grub!" said Bakugo, who promptly marched off, leaving Midoriya all alone.

Actually, it's hard to imagine sitting down for an actual meal with Kacchan.

The two boys had known each other since childhood, and for almost as long as Midoriya could remember, he'd been the persecuted, and Bakugo his persecutor. But that dynamic had slowly begun to change ever since they'd both gotten into U.A. High. They weren't exactly hanging out together the way they had as children, but it felt as if they were on more equal footing. Not that being alone with Bakugo was exactly a walk in the park, even these days.

Maybe just a sandwich from a convenience store…

After buying lunch and a drink, Midoriya started looking for a place to sit down and eat. The city streets were decorated for New Year's, although the boys had been too focused on patrolling to spare a second thought for the festive atmosphere. With that in mind, Midoriya hoped to find a quieter spot for his break.

Oh, how about by the shrine?

Midoriya scanned the map in his head and zeroed in on a shrine in the neighborhood, just a few minutes' walk away. It was a tranquil little oasis in the urban setting but still big enough to host seasonal events. In fact, when Midoriya arrived, he found that the shrine was full of festive stalls and locals milling about. Clearly it was a beloved getaway when one needed a break from big-city living.

"Oh, right! We're still in the middle of the hatsumode period," said Midoriya to himself, referencing the Japanese custom of making a special visit to a Shinto shrine or Buddhist temple during the first three days of the New Year. The clinking of coins in the offering box and the ringing of bells reminded Midoriya that he hadn't done his own hatsumode visit yet, so this seemed as good a chance as any.

"You ever gonna quit stalking me?" came a voice.

"Huh? Kacchan?"

The scowling Bakugo held his own plastic bag—presumably with lunch from a convenience store—and had apparently had the same thought about checking the shrine visit off his to-do list.

"Just a coincidence, I swear!" said Midoriya.

"Then why d'you keep popping up wherever I go?!" roared Bakugo, who clearly didn't appreciate sharing a train of thought with his longtime acquaintance.

"Keep it down, Kacchan! Let these good people celebrate New Year's in peace," said Midoriya, suddenly aware that the crowd was disturbed, presumably by Bakugo's howling.

"S'not me! It's *them* causing a scene!"

"Huh? 'Them' who?"

Midoriya followed Bakugo's pointing finger to the shrine's main structure, where the crowd was focused on a different pair of shouting boys.

"Quit messing around!"

"I'm not! Just listen to me!"

Midoriya and Bakugo approached the source of the commotion and found two boys arguing. Fifth or sixth graders, by the looks of them.

"You're just a big traitor, Macchan! Can't trust you as far as I can kick you!"

"It's 'as far as I can *toss* you,' Takkun! Not *kick*!"

"W-whatever! That's just atlantics!"

"You mean *semantics*?"

Though the exchange might have come off as a two-man comedy routine, it was clear that Macchan and Takkun weren't joking around. The gaffe-prone Takkun was red in the face from anger and embarrassment, and the more well-read Macchan was on the verge of tears.

Midoriya stepped forward, hoping to end the conflict.

"Take it easy, you two. Want to tell me what's going on?"

"Buzz off, brocco-head!" said Takkun.

"Geez, Takkun!" said Macchan.

Without a proverbial leg to stand on, Takkun desperately made a break for it past Midoriya, who was stunned into silence by the verbal lashing from a complete stranger. The boy didn't get far though, as he bumped straight into Bakugo, who was still grinning at "brocco-head."

"Going somewhere?" said Bakugo.

"Eek!" said Takkun. The little hellion tried to change course, but Bakugo's hand shot out and nabbed his shirt collar.

"Not even a 'sorry'? Were you raised by wolves?" asked Bakugo.

"Sh-shut up! Villain-face!"

The insult made Bakugo drop his guard, giving Takkun the opportunity to dash off.

"Takkun..." lamented Macchan, watching his companion vanish from sight. "Now what'm I gonna do about the hero *karuta* tournament tomorrow?" With a wail, he started crying, and despite Midoriya's attempts to console the boy, the tears flowed as if a levee had burst inside.

"Let the crybaby deal with his own problems," said Bakugo, but Midoriya guided Macchan to a bench set apart from the plaza and waited for the boy to stop crying. A reluctant Bakugo plopped himself down on the next bench over and dug into his own sandwich. By the time he took his last bite, Macchan's tears had stopped flowing, at which point Midoriya offered the child the drink he'd just bought.

"Mom says not to accept stuff from strangers..." said Macchan, looking wary.

"Sorry, of course! Well, I'm Deku, and this here is Kacchan."

"Nobody introduces me but *me*!" snapped Bakugo.

"Do you know Endeavor's hero agency? We're doing a work study over there, as trainees," explained Midoriya.

"Trainees...?" said Macchan. "So, you're gonna be heroes someday?"

"Exactly, so you can trust us. I'm sure all that crying dried you out, so drink this," said Midoriya.

"Okay. Thanks," said Macchan, whose nerves had been calmed by Midoriya's earnest approach.

"Now, can you tell me why you and your friend were fighting?" asked Midoriya.

Freshly hydrated, Macchan hesitated before speaking.

"Um, well... I'm gonna transfer to another school soon," he began, telling the full story slowly, bit by bit. It turned out that the two boys had been friends for years, but Macchan hadn't informed Takkun of his family's upcoming move. He'd finally confessed the sad news today, and Takkun hadn't reacted well.

"Hah," said Bakugo with a snort. "That whole tantrum, over that? Your pal's got some growing up to do."

"Hang on..." said Midoriya. "Did you mention a hero karuta tournament before?"

"Yeah, it's happening tomorrow, right here. Takkun and I were gonna enter together," said Macchan, pointing to a nearby poster advertising the event.

"Hero karuta... Now that brings me back!" said Midoriya, his eyes growing wide. Similar to the standard karuta card game, hero karuta was a race to slap the right card (one of many, in a face-up pile on the floor) based on the pro hero description called out by the reciter.

"Wait, you've played before, mister?" asked Macchan.

"Not in a tournament or anything!" said Midoriya. "Just at home, while my mom would read out the phrases."

"Oh, okay..." said Macchan, not nearly as excited as a moment ago. "I can't believe Takkun's just gonna skip the tournament, after we practiced so hard... Maybe I'll never even see him again..."

Tears started to fill Macchan's eyes again. Despite Midoriya's attempts to cheer him up, the boy remained in an inconsolable funk for the remainder of lunchtime, and then Midoriya had no choice but to leave with a hurried goodbye.

U.A.

When patrol ended that night, the three boys returned to Endeavor's agency—an ostentatious building that towered over some of the city's prime real estate. For the massive agency's thirty-plus sidekicks (alias: the Flaming Sidekickers), employment came with extensive perks, including a training gym, employee lodging, a cafeteria, and much, much more. Midoriya and his classmates had also been sleeping at the agency for the duration of their work study. After reporting on the day's events, they were headed to the cafeteria when they bumped into Burnin, one of Endeavor's sidekicks, who was carrying her emptied dinner tray.

"Hard day's work? How'd it go?" she asked. "I hope you're managing to keep up with the boss!"

"Stuff it," said Bakugo with a glare, while Midoriya and Todoroki nodded at her politely. On closer inspection, Burnin noticed how bedraggled and exhausted the trio looked.

"Nuh-uh, we don't let our people starve around here! Go get yourselves some *katsu* curry! It's the daily special!" said Burnin as she walked away.

Without a word to each other, the trio found an empty table, ordered their food (jumbo katsu curry for Midoriya, jumbo spicy katsu curry for Bakugo, and katsu curry with a side order of soba for Todoroki), and got to work on filling their empty stomachs, knowing that a hearty meal was just the thing to recover from the day's fatigue and give them strength for tomorrow. Bakugo left an empty seat between himself and Todoroki, ensuring that he'd be as far from Midoriya as possible. About halfway through the meal, Todoroki finally found the energy to strike up a conversation.

"Did you two try that book?" he asked.

"You mean *Meta Liberation War*?" said Midoriya. "Yeah, but I haven't finished yet, since I always fall asleep so quickly every night."

Meta Liberation War was one part autobiography, one part manifesto, written by Destro, the first leader of a radical faction that sought the right to use Quirks (or "meta abilities," as they were called in his days) more freely in society. Hawks, who was currently undercover

in the Paranormal Liberation Front, had handed Endeavor and the trio copies of the book, though the boys were none the wiser that Endeavor's copy contained a secret code from Hawks.

"Why the hell would I read anything by some extremist whack job?" said Bakugo. "And also, shut up—I'm trying to eat over here."

"Have you gotten through it, Todoroki?" asked Midoriya.

"No. I always nod off too," said Todoroki.

"Mm-hm. Once my head hits that pillow, it's game over. Oh, unrelated, but have you figured out that thing about condensing your power to a point?" said Midoriya.

"Not yet. I feel like I'm getting close, though... What about you, Bakugo?" said Todoroki.

"Course I've got the gist. And would you cram it, already?"

"Sorry," said Todoroki, who got back to slurping his soba noodles.

"You really love soba, don't you," said Midoriya.

"Yes. There's nothing more delicious," said Todoroki.

"Good thing you can add a soba side order to just about anything on the menu here, huh," said Midoriya. Besides the usual suspects like curry and various *donburi*, the menu offered sandwiches, pizza, cake, and other dishes that one wouldn't typically pair with soba.

Midoriya's observation prompted Kido and Onima—two more members of the Flaming Sidekickers—to pipe up from the table behind the boys.

"Heh, you noticed? There's actually a reason why they offer soba with *everything* here!" said Kido.

"After Shoto did his internship with us, the boss insisted on that change to the menu," explained Onima.

Todoroki instinctively scowled upon hearing this. The day their work study had formally begun, he'd said, "Let's stop that father-son crap in front of my friends," but every day was full of constant reminders that he was the boss's son. The murderous look forming on Todoroki's face—which Midoriya recognized—was reminiscent of the days when his obsessive hatred for Endeavor had isolated him from his peers and made him more than a little antisocial. But one look at the soba was enough to calm his nerves.

"Not the soba's fault, I guess," he said. The loud slurping resumed, and Midoriya breathed a sigh of relief. Bakugo shot a repulsed glance at Todoroki before reaching for more hot sauce for his curry.

"And he's actually pretty amazing, as a hero," added Todoroki. He still couldn't respect Enji Todoroki as a father, but he was plenty impressed by Endeavor, the pro hero. Working with the man in the field had only reaffirmed that assessment, and it was a stance that Midoriya and Bakugo shared.

"Ooh! The boss could die happy after hearing that!" said Onima.

"We'll have to pass on the compliment later!" said Kido.

"Don't. Please don't," said Todoroki. He'd already expressed that very sentiment to his father in person a while back, and he didn't need these sidekicks gossiping and stirring the pot any further.

Kido and Onima finished their meal, leaving the boys to themselves again.

"It's crazy how quickly Endeavor senses when there's trouble afoot, though. It's like he's got a built-in radar for these things," said Midoriya.

"Mm-hm. No matter how close we are to the perp, he always beats us to the punch," said Todoroki.

Midoriya had just been trying to make conversation, but Todoroki's frank response made him dive into his usual analysis mode.

"I used to have this image of him as a hero who would take down criminals through sheer force, but actually, there's much more subtlety to his moves. Maybe those instincts come from years of hero work? But it's not just that! His eye for detail extends to an impressive knack for crisis management, which I think we have to thank for the low crime stats here, within his jurisdiction. His big finisher moves might look flashy and haphazard, but a closer look has shown me how precise he is when he unleashes them. Audaciously delicate, you might say? I was also shocked at how spot-on his advice for us was. Being able to put pointers into words like that comes not just from instinct, but from hard work and experience, I think… Ah, not that I've got anything against learning by intuition, or…"

"SHUT! UP! Can't a guy eat in silence?"

"Oops, sorry, Kacchan!"

Midoriya was silenced by Bakugo for a moment, but his motormouth wouldn't be held at bay for long.

"Actually, since forever ago, I've noticed how you prefer silence when you're eating spicy food. And then, that one time in elementary school, you were like, 'Curry's not s'posed to be this sweet, dammit!' and the teacher got really mad."

"What did I *just* say? Maybe you'll pipe down with that katsu stuffed down your throat!" said Bakugo, reaching for Midoriya's plate.

"Whoa! Cut it out, Kacchan!" said Midoriya, trying to keep Bakugo from making good on that threat.

"You brought it on yourself!"

"Aren't you two childhood friends? Why do you fight so much?" said Todoroki, watching the madness with a puzzled expression.

"Huhh?"

"Hmm?"

"You've known each other for years, right?" said Todoroki. "I thought childhood friends were supposed to...act like actual friends."

While Midoriya struggled to come up with an answer to Todoroki's candid question, Bakugo's face twitched and contorted.

"What? As if you're s'posed to get along just cuz you've known someone awhile...? Then how d'you explain you and dear daddy, huh?"

Bakugo's pointed remark made Todoroki stop and think.

"No, you're right. After all, Midoriya and I are friends," he said.

"Aw, Todoroki..." said Midoriya with joy in his eyes. He hadn't made friends who really acted like friends until high school, so Todoroki's declaration delighted the former loner.

"That buddy-buddy crap makes me wanna hurl, so leave me the hell outta it!" howled Bakugo.

UA

After dinner, the three boys moved to the shared bathing area. While scrubbing away the dirt and grime, they chatted about the day's events, reflected on what

could've gone better, and discussed the kakizome homework. Their living quarters were equipped with personal showers, but one of the big perks of the extravagant agency was the bathing facility, which, like a hot spring resort, offered multiple types of baths to soothe weary bodies and strip away fatigue.

Patrol would begin bright and early the next morning, but any remaining time between bathing and bed was theirs to use as they wished. On this particular night, Midoriya spent some time studying with Todoroki before returning to his own room. He settled into the ample, inviting bed, but his eyes refused to close.

I hope those kids are okay...

That other pair of childhood friends was on his mind, and Midoriya was bothered by the fact that he hadn't been able to declare "I'm sure you'll make up in no time" to Macchan. What right did he have to give that sort of pep talk without experience to back it up?

"Aren't you two childhood friends? Why do you fight so much?"

Midoriya sighed, remembering Todoroki's reasonable question.

He and Bakugo had played together as kids, but that had all changed out of the blue one day, and Midoriya still had no inkling why. Even if they were on more even footing recently, that history couldn't be erased.

When asked, Midoriya would describe his relationship with Bakugo by saying they were childhood friends, but was that really apt? As Todoroki had pointed out, they didn't get along at all, and no outside observer would guess that they were friends now.

In contrast, the boys from earlier had been prepared to enter a karuta tournament together; there was genuine friendship there.

I just hope they patch things up somehow...

Midoriya tried running simulations in his head about how Macchan and Takkun might bury the hatchet, but there was no easy answer. Hoping to cool his overworked head, he got out of bed and made for the beverage corner.

"Kacchan?"

"If it ain't my stalker again."

Bakugo was sitting on a windowsill with a soda in hand. Unable to muster the strength for a retort or denial, Midoriya gave a weak, ambiguous chuckle

before fetching a beverage of his own. He thought about picking one of the health drinks loaded with protein but ultimately settled on mineral water to slake his thirst. Bakugo made no move to return to his own room, so Midoriya approached, being sure to leave a safe distance between them.

"I wonder if those boys will make it to the karuta tourney tomorrow," he said.

"Who cares? That's their business," said Bakugo.

"I...guess so, but..."

Midoriya had nothing to follow up with, so he just sipped his water while Bakugo gulped his soda.

"That little crybaby reminded me of another dork I know," said Bakugo with a slight sneer.

Midoriya realized the other dork was him. He had been a crybaby—that wasn't up for debate—but the fact that the jab annoyed him at all felt like proof that he wasn't the punching bag he'd once been.

"Yeah? Well, I saw a little bit of you in the other boy," said Midoriya.

"Huhh?! Which part?"

"The nasty mouth on him."

Bakugo remembered Takkun's "villain-face" comment and scowled.

"We ain't alike at all!" spat Bakugo, but the retort sounded half-hearted, as if he couldn't fully deny the resemblance. He hopped off the windowsill with a discontented cluck of his tongue, but as he walked past, Midoriya mumbled something under his breath.

"I just want them to make up…"

Bakugo stopped in his tracks.

"Quit acting so high 'n' mighty, like you know what's best for everyone."

"Huh?"

"You seriously got the energy to cry about brats you never even met before today? The way you do that kinda crap… It's always given me the freakin' creeps," said Bakugo with a seething glare. He stomped off, leaving Midoriya to breathe in the stinging silence left in his wake. It was an old but familiar sensation that made him sigh. Midoriya genuinely wished the best for those boys, but Bakugo only saw a hypocrite indulging in virtue signaling.

He forced the final sip of water down his throat, sighed again, and shuffled off to bed in preparation for another busy day.

UA

While out on patrol the next day, the boys could barely keep up with Endeavor, as usual.

"Deku!" shouted Endeavor. "Get your head outta the clouds! You're here to work, right?"

"Sorry, sir!"

Endeavor's scolding came after Midoriya had lagged behind while chasing down a villain. Try as he might, his lack of sleep was keeping him from focusing properly.

I wonder what happened with those boys and their karuta tournament... Ack! No, no—focus up. It's not like I can go and check up on them...

Midoriya had to remind himself that yesterday's leisurely lunch break had been the exception to the rule. But a few hours into their patrol shift, a miracle happened.

"What?" said Endeavor into his phone. "An emergency call from Mirko? Fine, patch her through."

"What's up, Endeavor? Mind lending me a hand or two? I'm dealing with a villain who doesn't know when to quit!"

Mirko—the unyielding bunny hero—was loud enough that the boys could hear her voice even without Endeavor's phone at their ears, which got Midoriya all sorts of excited. Apparently, she was facing a villain weak to fire Quirks, so when Endeavor agreed to help, she ended the call with *"Great! And make it snappy!"* without bothering to mention the location.

"Where does she get off..." said a grimacing Endeavor. After a pause, he changed gears and gave the boys orders.

"I would tell you three 'Keep up!' but in an emergency like this, you'd only slow me down. Until I get back, keep patrolling with the sidekicks."

With lightning-quick judgment, Endeavor realized that if habitual solo artist Mirko was having trouble, then this villain was probably no laughing matter. "Lemme come too!" protested Bakugo, but Endeavor

was already fading into the distance, which further fueled Bakugo's bad mood.

As luck would have it, there were no incidents for the rest of the morning, so Midoriya and Bakugo were granted a rare lunch break once again, while Todoroki returned to the agency for a follow-up to the interview of the day before. Of course, they were still technically on call, just in case an emergency popped up.

"Kacchan, I'm gonna head to that shrine for... Wait, huh?"

Before he could explain that he wanted to check out the hero karuta tournament, Midoriya realized Bakugo was already gone.

Probably ran off to get some lunch?

Midoriya hurried back to the shrine on his own and found the place bustling with friends and family of the tournament entrants.

Now where are those boys? Did they even show up today?

Midoriya scanned the crowd and instantly noticed a familiar spiky hairdo.

"Kacchan!"

"Tch!"

Bakugo clucked his tongue without even bothering to turn around and acknowledge Midoriya.

"What brings you here, huh?" asked Midoriya. "Don't tell me you also care about those boys!"

"I was just hoping to find those food stalls from yesterday, is all!"

"Oh. Right," said Midoriya, who knew from Bakugo's pinched expression that getting any closer to him would end badly. That was then they both heard a pair of familiar voices.

"We gotta play, though! What was all that practice for?"

"No way!"

"Then why'd you even come here?"

It was Macchan and Takkun, arguing near the registration table. Takkun didn't have a clever answer for Macchan's reasonable question, so he lashed out in desperation.

"I-I wanted to watch you cry and be all sad that you couldn't join the tourney!"

Midoriya and Bakugo realized that was the best bluff Takkun could muster, but Macchan took the words at face value and seemed genuinely hurt.

"Aw, man…" said Takkun, suddenly regretting his own cruelty.

"Hey, you two," said Midoriya, walking up to them. "So you're playing in the tournament after all? Why don't we all calm down and talk this out…"

He'd butted in with the best intentions, but a second later, Midoriya found his arm tugged by Macchan.

"Actually, I'm entering with this guy now!" he said. "So you can buzz off, Takkun!"

"Huh?"

Midoriya hadn't expected to become part of a triangle like this, and Takkun was equally stunned.

"Well, ain't it your goddamned lucky day!" said Bakugo wryly. "Helping people out is a hero's job, *riiight*?"

"Th-then my partner's gonna be villain-face over here!" declared Takkun, who wrapped his arms around one of Bakugo's.

"What? Why me?"

"Why so reluctant, Kacchan? We're supposed to be heroes, *aren't we*?" said Midoriya.

"I ain't shooting for hero status just to join a card game with some brat!" said Bakugo, ripping his arm away to show he meant it.

"What the heck!" said Takkun in a panic. "I-I guess you never played hero karuta before! Yeah, that must be it!"

"That game for babies? Sure haven't," said Bakugo without missing a beat.

"Dang, with a mean ol' face like that, I was sure you'd be great at it, but...you're a total scrub? We're gonna lose so bad!"

Little did Takkun know that in his despair, he'd uttered just the right words to light a fire under Bakugo, who felt a pathological need to be a winner at all things.

"Lose? If you think I'd lose at this kiddie game, you got another thing coming!"

And with that, the teams were decided—Midoriya and Macchan versus Bakugo and Takkun. And as luck would have it, the drawing of lots determined that they would be squaring off in round one of the tournament, doubles-style. Atop a tatami mat, each boy sat on his knees next to his partner, and between the pairs was a scattered pile of cards adorned with images of heroes.

"You get how this works, right, villain-face?" asked Takkun. "When they read out a hero phrase, you gotta touch the right card fastest to win it for your team.

Okay?" The boy sounded concerned as he explained the rules to his new partner.

"Touch the right card fastest, blah, blah, blah. Sounds easy," said Bakugo dismissively. Across from him sat Midoriya, who nodded when Macchan whispered "Good luck!" to him.

"You're that confident, Kacchan?"

"Huh?"

Something in Midoriya's voice didn't sit easy with Bakugo. Intuitively, he sensed impending disaster, took his first good look at the cards, and realized why he was in trouble—the cards didn't have a smidge of writing on them. Midoriya saw the gears turning in Bakugo's head.

"That's right," said Midoriya ominously. "Unlike in regular karuta, the cards in hero karuta have no words, just pictures. Plus, each round's selection is chosen randomly from the full set of several hundred, and some of the descriptions start with the same word. If you can't immediately recognize which hero corresponds to the phrase they read out, you'll never win a single card, which means..."

"You gotta memorize all the stupid phrases first?" said Bakugo.

"S'why I said a beginner would lose at this game!" said Takkun.

"You coulda explained that earlier!" came Bakugo's retort.

"What the heck, villain-face! You signed yourself up before I could explain anything!" said Takkun.

"Takkun..." lamented Macchan, as he and Midoriya watched Bakugo and Takkun's spat with concern.

I just wanted these boys to be friends again, but now we're caught up in the battle ourselves...

"Let round one begin!" declared the reciter. Midoriya braced for the first hero description.

I'm mostly here as a seat filler, so I should let Macchan take the lead and...

"Cr—"

With a deafening slap and a mind of its own, Midoriya's hand shot out and landed on a card near the edge of the arena. The reciter was stunned silent for a moment before managing to finish the phrase.

"Crime will soon cease, thanks to the Symbol of Peace..."

"The card's mine!" said Midoriya, having won the All Might card. "Oh. Oops?"

The casual practice with his mother had apparently paid off, since Midoriya had memorized every last phrase to the letter. He was suddenly wary of seeming like a show-off, but Macchan practically had stars in his eyes.

"Wow! I couldn't even see your hand, it moved so fast!" said the boy.

"S-sorry!" said Midoriya. "That's my favorite card by far, so I couldn't help myself..."

"Don't be sorry! Winning the cards is a good thing! I just gotta try to keep up!" said Macchan.

"Sure!" said Midoriya, now convinced by Macchan's earnest smile that he hadn't done anything wrong. Meanwhile, Bakugo's and Takkun's jaws were still on the floor.

"Damn nerd!" said Bakugo, his jaw snapping back into position and twisting into a snarl.

"W-what the heck!" said Takkun, pointing at Midoriya. "You didn't say your new partner was so good, Macchan! You bustler!"

"I didn't know either!" fired back Macchan. "And it's *hustler*, not *bustler*. *Bustler* is just, like...someone doing errands in a big hurry, or something!"

"Urgh!"

Left without a retort once again, Takkun could only chew on his lip and stew in fury.

"Do you boys mind if we continue?" asked the reciter.

"Sorry, yes, please go ahead!" said a mortified Midoriya. When playing for fun with his mother, he'd only loosely stuck to the rules, but a formal match like this was a serious affair. The more serious the game, the sweeter the victory in the end.

"Next card..." said the reciter. "His v—"

Another loud smack, this time from Macchan's hand, which had landed on the Present Mic card.

"...oice echoes far, past the moon and the stars."

"Good going, Macchan!" said Midoriya. Macchan beamed, while across from him, Takkun frowned and grumbled to himself.

"Darn... I'll get this next one!"

However...

Slap!

Slap!

Slap!

Midoriya and Macchan racked up the cards, one after the other, and despite Bakugo's and Takkun's attempts,

they were always an instant behind. Bakugo's beginner status explained the trouble he was having, but the skill gap between Macchan and Takkun was pretty massive, considering that they'd trained together. Eventually coming to realize this himself, Takkun balled his fists and grew unusually quiet. Midoriya was trying to figure out how to encourage the boy when Bakugo stepped in.

"Listen, you little turd! Do you wanna win or not?"

"Course I wanna win! Duh!"

"How're you gonna smack cards with those fists, huh?"

Takkun gasped and glared back at Bakugo.

"Shaddup, villain-face! I was just about to open my hands again, dummy!" said Takkun.

"You brat! Is that any way to talk to people?!" said Bakugo, ignoring his own blatant hypocrisy. Before Takkun could fire back again, the reciter harrumphed, prompting the panicked boy to shut up and get into position. This time, there was fire in Takkun's eyes.

"Next card..." said the reciter. "Fla—"

Takkun slapped a card right in front of him.

"...mes say your prayers, whether up- or down-stairs."

An excited Takkun held the Backdraft card in his hand.

"Why didn'tcha play like that from the start?" said Bakugo, his venomous tone stripping the compliment of all the good will it might otherwise have had.

"Just sit back and relax, villain-face," said Takkun. "I'm good enough to play for the both of us."

"Got a big head now, do ya?"

Rage flashed in Bakugo's eyes as they swiveled to focus on the cards.

"A worldw—"

Bakugo's open hand descended with shocking speed onto the Best Jeanist card.

"...ide fashion star, from Monaco to Myanmar."

"You actually knew that one, Kacchan?" asked a dumbfounded Midoriya.

"Nope," said Bakugo with a haughty snort. "But there ain't a ton of heroes in the mix who do anything 'worldwide.'"

Best Jeanist was actually missing in action at the moment, but before his disappearance, the denim-clad hero had moonlighted as a fashion model with top clothing brands all over the world. The previous year,

Bakugo had been scouted by Best Jeanist for an internship, mostly because the hero hoped to correct Bakugo's notoriously bad attitude.

In any case, Takkun gazed at Bakugo with an aura of newfound respect—duly impressed by that deductive reasoning.

"Villain-face... You're not half bad..."

"Hah. If that knocked your socks off, then you just wait," said Bakugo.

"My—"

Slap!

"Her—"

Slap!

"Aca—"

Slap!

Bakugo and Takkun continued to rack up the cards, but Midoriya and Macchan were unfazed, because they knew that games like this had an ebb and flow to them. For now, they were calmly observing their opponents while saving their energy for the cards that remained. Their patience paid off.

"The bu—"

Slap! Macchan's hand came down hard on the Mirko card.

"…nny that leaped over the moon is sure to make you swoon."

Macchan's streak continued with the cards for Midnight ("Whatever the time of day, Midnight's ready to play"), Yoroi Musha ("Nothing mushy about his code of Bushido"), Uwabami ("Bad hair days are headaches when you're dealing with snakes"), Endeavor ("His fiery frame has won him acclaim"), Ryukyu ("Rumor's a'buzzin' she's got a dino for a cousin"), Hawks ("About his red wings he's cocky, and we're not talking hockey"), and Edgeshot ("Stealth is his art—he'll infiltrate your heart").

Despite Takkun's best efforts, he just couldn't keep up with his friend's quick reflexes. But he wasn't willing to back down, even in the face of a widening point gap.

"This ain't over yet! Victory's gonna be mine in the end," said Takkun, slapping both of his own cheeks to hype himself up. Midoriya caught a note of melancholy on Macchan's face at the words "in the end."

"Ma—"

Slap!

"Pr—"

Slap!

Takkun had once again taken control, and the match was nearing its end. But despite the shrinking pile of cards and the growing point gap, Macchan showed no signs of panic. Midoriya realized something was off.

Hold on, is he...?

Bakugo also raised an eyebrow suspiciously.

"Tr—"

Macchan and Takkun both reached for a card closer to Macchan's side. Takkun touched it first, but only because Macchan's hand had frozen in place, just above the card. Takkun stared in horror.

"Macchan, you...you...you're using kid mittens on me!" said Takkun.

"A-am not..." said Macchan. Unable to look Takkun in the eye, he didn't even bother correcting *kid mittens* to *kid gloves*. Takkun's face flushed red with rage.

"It's kid *gloves*. Get it right, dummy," said Bakugo, filling in for Macchan.

"Shut up, shut up, shut up..." whined Takkun with tears in his eyes, his anger leaving him without a proper comeback.

Frustration at someone caring a little too much was something Bakugo understood all too well. Midoriya might've claimed to act out of the goodness of his heart, but to Bakugo, that cloying, "golly gee!" brand of caring came off as a sickening, holier-than-thou attitude. For the life of him, he couldn't comprehend people who acted out of a simple desire to help others, with no ulterior motive. Midoriya was the childhood "friend" whom Bakugo just couldn't shake, and to him, it felt like Midoriya's constant presence was somehow messing with Bakugo's destiny.

"And *you*…" said Bakugo, about to chew into Macchan for holding back. But he was interrupted.

"That's not right. You have to play seriously," said Midoriya, gently but firmly. "Sometimes an honest match can teach you things you never realized."

Macchan looked up at his doubles partner in shock. Under Midoriya's serious gaze, the boy suddenly felt a pang of guilt.

"Right…" he said with a nod, turning to Takkun. "Sorry for taking it easy on you."

"Yeah? No more mittens… I mean, gloves. Kid gloves. No more of that," said Takkun.

"Okay!" said Macchan.

The boys smiled at each other, as if to say, "No hard feelings." Midoriya was overcome with relief, which didn't go unnoticed by Bakugo.

In the aftermath of All Might's sudden and forced retirement, the guilt over Bakugo's role in those events had eaten away at him. When he couldn't take it anymore, he'd summoned Midoriya for a heart-to-heart one night, which had transformed into full-on battle between the boys and their troubled souls. It was their first honest-to-goodness, no-holds-barred fight, and ever since, that sickening feeling in Bakugo's stomach had begun to wane. Still, it was hard to put his finger on what it was about Midoriya that still gave him the creeps. The haughty purity about him? That drive to become a hero solely for the purpose of helping others? Bakugo just couldn't understand it, but he was starting to accept that fact. That awareness had gone a long way toward helping him endure Midoriya's presence.

"This match is a true battle, and you'd better win!" said Bakugo, slapping Takkun on the back.

"Yeah, for sure!" said Takkun.

"Let's keep focused until the very end!" said Midoriya, encouraging Macchan.

"Okay!" said Macchan.

The reciter, who'd been watching this whole affair play out, made a throat-clearing noise.

"May we go on?"

"Ah, sorry about all the delays, really!" said Midoriya. He, Macchan, and Takkun bowed to the reciter, and the game continued.

The rest of the match played out fair and square, and Midoriya and Macchan eked out a narrow victory. This earned them a chance to compete in round two, where they lost to a pair who'd been trained in the art of hero karuta from the time they were old enough to slap cards.

"Dang! Those demon twins are just too good!" said Takkun, as if he'd been the one who'd lost.

Macchan smiled at his friend.

"Wait, why're you so happy about losing?" asked Takkun.

"Cuz it's proof that I gave it my all against you, Tak-kun," said Macchan. "Not holding back...makes me feel really good. So thanks for the help, Deku."

"I'm just glad you see it that way," said Midoriya, returning Macchan's smile.

"Plus," said Macchan, addressing Takkun again, "our match against you guys was so exciting. With all that back-and-forth...it was hard to guess who was gonna win. Especially when it came down to just Ingenium and Fat Gum, since both their phrases start with 'If...'! That threw me off!"

"Man, I even guessed that one right, but you still won! You're just too good at this, Macchan," said Tak-kun, with a sad smile. Macchan shook his head—as if to chase the sad vibes away—and put on a brave face.

"Takkun!" he said. "I know I'm going to a new school, but I'm gonna keep playing hero karuta, okay? I'm never gonna quit! So...we'll play together again someday, right?"

"G-guess you're not giving me a choice! Fine, let's make a pinkie contract!" said Takkun.

"You mean *pinkie promise*? Oh, whatever. Close enough!"

"You're always getting strung up on the details, Macchan."

The two young boys locked pinkie fingers and thanked Midoriya and Bakugo for their help. As they ran off, Midoriya grinned and waved goodbye, while Bakugo clucked his tongue.

"There goes our precious lunch break," said Bakugo.

"Ack! I forgot about the 'lunch' part!" said Midoriya. Before he could leave, he remembered something and swiveled back toward the shrine.

"I still haven't done a proper hatsumode visit yet! You go on ahead without me, Kacchan," he said.

"Dammit, Deku! S'not my style to let you beat me at anything!" said Bakugo, as he dashed past Midoriya. They were only a few paces from the shrine to start with, so they wound up praying side by side anyway.

"Well, what'd you wish for?" asked Midoriya.

"For you to shut up," said Bakugo.

Bakugo looked as grumpy as ever, but something earnest in his eyes made Midoriya suspect that their wishes had probably overlapped.

Winning to save. Saving to win. Becoming the top hero.

They couldn't have been further apart, personality-wise, and they saw the world in completely different ways. "Cats and dogs" didn't even begin to describe how poorly these two got along, and yet Midoriya couldn't imagine a world without Bakugo. Even those horrible memories had shaped him into the person he was today, which had eventually led to his fateful encounter with All Might. Yes, Midoriya had made it this far thanks to the people in his life, so he was going to walk this path as far as it could take him. All these thoughts and realizations swirled around in his head, forming a renewed sense of resolve.

"Midoriya? Bakugo? I didn't know you were here," came a voice from behind.

It was Todoroki, who had decided to visit the same shrine after his lunch meeting.

"Oh. You're getting along now?" he asked, noticing his classmates standing side by side.

The childhood friends took a second to respond.

"Say something that disgusting again, and I'll blast the teeth right outta your mouth!" said Bakugo, who was getting goose bumps at the very thought of "getting along" with Midoriya.

"I'm afraid not, Todoroki," said a pale Midoriya, somberly.

"Oh. Okay…?" said a clearly puzzled Todoroki, just as Midoriya's phone rang.

"*Deku! Break's over! Is Bakugo with you?*" asked one of the sidekicks.

"Y-yes! I've got Kacchan and Todoroki with me right here! We're on our way!" replied a panicked Midoriya, whose legs were already moving.

"Come on, guys! They want us back!" he said, prompting Bakugo to cluck his tongue as he and Todoroki started running, their breath white and visible in the chilly winter air. This was the path of the hero, and their winter break would be over in just a few short days.

A n extravagant New Year's party was unfolding in the banquet hall of the castle-like Yaoyorozu mansion. It was a yearly to-do that drew over three hundred guests from the Yaoyorozu family's elite social circles, and Momo Yaoyorozu—the daughter of the family—was dressed up to the nines as she went around greeting the party guests.

"I hear you're enrolled at none other than U.A. High, Momo," said one partygoer.

"You've heard correctly," said Momo. "U.A. is the best institution around for instilling self-discipline, though I still have a long way to go."

The casual small talk came effortlessly to Momo, who'd been attending these shindigs since before she could remember. These experiences mingling with high society might even come in handy someday, if she ever had to infiltrate a fancy function for a hero mission.

Any moment now, I suspect…

The Yaoyorozu New Year's party always featured a presentation or performance by an artist or entertainer of some sort, and it was one element of the night that Momo always looked forward to. As she wondered what the evening's entertainment might be, the lights suddenly dimmed, and a spotlight shone on Mr. Yaoyorozu, who stood atop the banquet hall's stage. Momo's father was looking as suave and put together as ever.

"Friends and family," he began, "I know this is a moment you've all been waiting for, but instead of the usual catered entertainment, we've hastily thrown together a special *film* for you this evening."

A film? Of what, I wonder?

Momo had been out of the loop concerning this year's party planning since U.A.'s decision to send the students home at all had been rather last-minute. Now, the massive screen that lowered over the stage only piqued her excitement further.

"Put together by an Academy Award–winning director, this short film chronicles the path thus far of our beloved daughter, from birth to present. I give you *The History of Momo Yaoyorozu*!"

"Huh?" gasped Momo, taken aback.

The film's title appeared on the screen with a bam, accompanied by a dramatic, sweeping soundtrack. The first scene seemed to be about Momo's parents falling in love, but she was too busy marching away to see much. Off to the side of the stage, she found her parents standing with their head butler, who'd been with the family since before Momo was born.

"Father! Care to explain the meaning of this?" she asked.

"Surprised, are you?" said Mr. Yaoyorozu. "That school of yours didn't leave us very much time to put this together."

"Though I must say, the director was delighted at the opportunity," added Mrs. Yaoyorozu with a broad smile.

"I'm not concerned about the details," said a flustered Momo. "I'm asking why you've commissioned such a thing in the first place!"

"Because we want these good people to know just how wonderful you are, naturally," said her father.

The movie had moved on to a scene featuring a newborn Momo, which elicited cheers and murmers of "Aww!" from the audience. Momo felt as if her parents had sat the entire guest list down for a look at her baby photo albums. In a way, this was worse, but her father was blithely unaware of her embarrassment.

"That dormitory room they've stuck you in," he said, frowning. "It must be awfully cramped. I could hardly believe it when they forced you to mail all those boxes and furniture back home."

"Indeed," said Momo's mother. "They only allowed us to send a single cardboard box as a care package. Why, we could barely fit a collection of your favorite teas in there, let alone everything else you ought to have with you…"

"And I take it you have to endure, erm, *communal bathing*? I suppose you're in desperate need of a private soak after so long, no?" said Mr. Yaoyorozu. Suddenly his face lit up with a flash of inspiration.

"I know! We could have a spa built on the U.A. campus! Patrons could reserve bathing times, giving you some privacy and helping the students of U.A. to battle their fatigue."

"Oh, that sounds lovely, doesn't it?" said Mrs. Yaoyorozu. "And how about a shopping mall to match? Then you could purchase whatever you might need, at any time."

"Brilliant, my dear! Why not amusement facilities as well? Work hard, play hard, as the people say! I'll draw up the plans at once and bring the proposal to that diminutive principal!"

"Father!"

Momo's piercing shout stunned her garrulous parents into silence.

"Whatever is the matter?" asked her father, at which Momo narrowed her eyes and pursed her lips.

"I...appreciate the sentiment, I do. But my U.A. experience is not lacking anything," she explained.

"But..."

"They say that home is where one hangs one's hat, even if that happens to be a, erm, *cozy* dorm room. And quite frankly, bathing with the other girls presents an opportunity for meaningful communication. As for shopping, yes—I may feel inconvenienced now and then—but the school store offers the essentials. And living in a dorm provides endless entertainment in the form of conversation with classmates. Every day, I find myself learning new things from them. As it happens, I've been listening to a genre of music called 'metal,' lately. It was my friend Jiro who opened my eyes to it—or ears, I suppose—while I've enjoyed the honor and privilege of introducing her to classical music, meager though my knowledge may be. These seemingly trivial things add up to a valuable experience...and one that truly makes me happy. All of which is to say, I'm quite satisfied with my life at U.A. High, thank you very much."

Momo's parents seemed at once shocked and dejected by their daughter's sincere, impassioned defense of U.A.

"Very well... We only have the best intentions, but I suppose we shouldn't meddle," said her father.

"Momo... I'm afraid we were so excited to finally have you back home that we got ahead of ourselves. Apologies..." said her mother.

"Mother, Father... Oh dear..." said Momo, suddenly fearing that she'd been too harsh.

"Miss Momo," interjected the butler, "your parents are simply concerned about your first communal living experience, to the extent that they lose sleep over it. Do try to understand that."

"Is that true?" asked Momo, turning back to her parents.

"What sort of parents would we be if we weren't worried about you?" said her father.

"In fact," said her mother, "your father has been musing about moving into a property next door to U.A."

"You're one to talk! You've been in the habit of covering the bed with Momo's earliest *matryoshka* dolls and burying yourself in the pile."

"You want to talk matryoshka? I know for a fact that you sometimes *speak* to them, as if they were your own daughter!"

"When did y... You saw that?"

Momo couldn't help but chuckle at her parents' back-and-forth. Meanwhile, up on the movie screen, a young Momo was playing in the gardens while her parents watched, their eyes unmistakably full of love. As she watched them bicker in real time about which of them missed her more, she sensed that same love, preserved and strengthened over the years.

To make them worry so much, though... Clearly I must learn be more considerate about these things.

It was a moment of reflection that led to newfound determination.

I shall have to grow competent enough for others to feel comfortable relying on me! So that they have no need to worry or fret!

That was when Momo suddenly remembered the kakizome assignment.

Why not 実力, (jitsuryoku) as "competence"?

"Momo?" asked her mother, who'd noticed Momo looking pensive.

"Oh, it's nothing, really. But I'm afraid I've missed a good portion of the film you made in my honor. May I watch it from the start, later?"

"Of course!" said her father.

"We can sit down with the staff for another screening," said her mother.

Momo smiled weakly at the thought of another public viewing as she turned to the screen. There, for all to see, young Momo was creating a matryoshka doll for the first time, beaming with satisfaction and pride.

Hot Pot Party to Get Fired Up!

The work studies had occupied the entire winter break, and the first day of the new school term had finally arrived.

Just as the students of class 1-A were about to give a practical demonstration on what they had learned and accomplished over the break, Aizawa and Present Mic had gotten a call from Gran Torino, summoning them to the prison known as Tartarus. The authorities had realized that Kurogiri—a member of the League of Villains—was likely a Nomu created from the dead body of Oboro Shirakumo, who had been Aizawa and Mic's friend during their own high school days at U.A. The two teachers had traveled to the prison where Kurogiri was held in hopes of finding out more, and the trip had paid off with a key hint concerning the Paranormal Liberation Front's plot.

Later that very day, Aizawa comforted Eri over her horn—which had begun to tingle—and gave a pep talk to All Might, who was feeling uneasy over Midoriya's recent growth. Meanwhile, the kids of class 1-A were all in their dorm building's common area, holding a work-study share session and hot pot party to fire them up for the new term. Then, their next-door neighbors showed up.

"Knock, knock!"

Still gathered around the hot pots, the members of class A turned to the front entrance to see the girls of class B walk through the door. Itsuka Kendo was in the lead, with Yui Kodai, Ibara Shiozaki, Kinoko Komori, Pony Tsunotori, Setsuna Tokage, and Reiko Yanagi in tow.

"Please, come on in!" said Tenya Ida, stepping into his role as class president. He, Momo Yaoyorozu, Ochaco Uraraka, and a few others moved toward the door to greet the newcomers with shouts of, "Welcome, welcome!" This was hardly the first interclass visit, so no one was feeling particularly shy about mingling.

"Here—a little something from us," said Kendo, handing Yaoyorozu a bag. "Just some drinks and snacks for after dinner."

"You really didn't have to!" said Yaoyorozu.

Denki Kaminari came running up to Kodai, who was carrying a few sofas that she'd shrunk with her Quirk.

"Lemme take those off your hands!" he said, stretching out his own hand in an overly eager attempt to look good in front of these girls.

"That's fine. We got this," said Yanagi, who used her "Poltergeist" Quirk to levitate the sofas out of Kodai's hands and toward the sitting area. Noticing this, Rikido Sato, Koji Koda, and Shoto Todoroki shifted the existing ottomans and sofas out of the way to make room. Yanagi lowered the new furniture into place, and Kodai grew it back to full size by releasing the effects of her Quirk. His attempt to impress foiled, the speechless Kaminari could only grin awkwardly.

"Swing and a miss, Kaminari!" said Minoru Mineta, who had seen right through his friend's intentions.

"Huhh? I'm a gentleman to everyone, though," protested Kaminari. Mineta shook his head and beckoned with one finger.

"Listen, buddy... Having more girls around is always ideal," he whispered.

"For real!" said Kaminari. "I want girls on every side of me! No dudes..."

"When I kick the bucket, I wanna be reincarnated as a hot pot..." said Mineta. "Think about it! Ladies on every side, all poking at you... Getting them all hot and bothered..."

"That would be...pretty great," said Kaminari.

The boys were too caught up in the fantasy to realize that Kyoka Jiro had overheard them.

"Morons," she said, clearly disgusted.

"Aw, come on. Can't a coupla guys dream?" said Kaminari.

"Dream? More like a nightmare," said Jiro, who felt an urge to protect the class B guests from her not-so-pure-minded classmates. Beside her, Tsuyu Asui suddenly looked toward the front door.

"Hmm? Will this be all of you?" she asked.

"Naw, the boys are coming too, of course," said Kendo. "Might take a minute...given what they're bringing. And seriously, class A—sorry in advance."

Class A wasn't sure how to react to that preemptive apology.

"Sorry about what?" asked Mina Ashido.

Katsuki Bakugo stopped eating for a second and looked like he'd swallowed something bitter.

"If class B's got something to be sorry about, you don't gotta guess twice about who's to blame," he said.

The rest of class A came to the same realization, and suddenly, as if he'd been waiting for this perfect timing to make his entrance, none other than class B's perennial troublemaker and class A hater came bursting through the door.

"Howdy! Kept you waiting, didn't I? Dying of anticipation, I bet?" said Neito Monoma, whose intense love for his own class B fueled a powerful rivalry with class A, at least in his own mind.

"No. Nobody here was dying of anything," said Todoroki, as he slurped down a string of chives that he'd chopped poorly. Ignoring the blunt retort, Monoma strolled into the building and practically skipped over to the bubbling hot pots on the table.

"There's enough food for everyone and then some, so please, enjoy!" said Ida, prompting Sato to hand out bowls and chopsticks to the guests. But it wasn't hunger that drove Monoma; the glint in his eyes was that of a critic.

"I see a soy milk hot pot," he began. "And kimchi, over there? Then we have a yosenabe...and *tan-tan* sesame? Do I have that right?"

Monoma had correctly identified class A's culinary creations, all four of which were fairly standard staples of the Japanese hot pot world. Each kid was sitting in front of his or her favorite of the four.

"Heh... A regular lineup of bog-standard clichés, I'd say," said Monoma.

"Whaddaya mean? These are quality dishes," said a troubled Sato—class A's unofficial head chef. He had overseen the preparation of every hot pot there, and he wasn't the type to offer guests anything subpar.

"Too true, Sato!" said Kaminari. "We all worked real hard on these guys, so you gotta try 'em before talking smack!"

"Kaminari... Do you really think I paid a visit to your den of inadequacy just to try hot pots made by class A, of all people?" said Monoma.

"Worry not!" said Ida, raising a hand emphatically. "We also plan to swap stories about our work studies in hopes of further edification!"

"All in good time... But I'm alluding to the hot pots prepared by class B! Ones far more delicious than these!" said Monoma.

Class A was stunned silent, and just then, the rest of the class B boys arrived at the front door. They hadn't come empty-handed.

"We got the goods, Monoma!" said Tetsutetsu Tetsutetsu.

"Why'd you get to make a solo entrance, huh?" asked Kosei Tsuburaba. These two newest arrivals were gingerly carrying a hot pot of their own, as were Juzo Honenuki and Yosetsu Awase.

"Pardon us!" said Honenuki. "Ah, don't worry about bowls and chopsticks. We brought our own."

"How thoughtful of you!" said Ida with a bow. "Oh, are those hot pots I spy? I assure you, we had already made enough for your class as well."

"Foolish class A..." said Monoma. "These hot pots are our way of throwing down the gauntlet! A competition is about to unfold, and we shall all learn whose concoctions are tastier!" He pointed a dismissive finger at class A's pots.

Seeing that the declaration of war had left class A confused, Kendo apologized again.

"Sorry, guys. He just doesn't listen to reason when he gets like this..."

Her weary smile hinted at her thankless role as Monoma's babysitter. Meanwhile, the class B boys had set their two pots on the table.

"Smells yummers!" said Uraraka, who was the closest thing class A had to a gourmand. Not missing a beat, Monoma leaned in close to her.

"Right? Right? Just imagine how delicious they taste!"

"Eek!" yelped Uraraka.

"Go on, then. Give them a try! ...Urk!"

A swift chop to the neck from Kendo put a temporary stop to Monoma's madness.

"Sorry again," said Kendo.

But Monoma was only out cold for a second; the sheer desire to see class A defeated seemed to animate his body and bring him back to life.

"Well?" he asked. "Shall we get this competition started?"

 SCHOOL BRIEFS

"Competition? Nonsense. Why don't we all just enjoy this meal?" suggested Ida.

"Ohh, I suppose you're all scared of losing to our hot pots. Tell me—are *you* scared, Bakugo?"

"Huh? Couldn't care less," answered Bakugo, not taking the obvious bait.

Having failed to light class A's shortest fuse, Monoma was at a momentary loss. During the battle training between the classes, he'd been caught off guard by Bakugo's growth, which he'd called "character development" at the time. Monoma was always one to think on his feet, however, so he now set his sights on the kimchi hot pot that Bakugo was enjoying.

"No, I'm afraid your cooking can't compete with ours in the least. Take that kimchi one, for instance. Looks to me like you've just tossed some kimchi in a pot and called it a day! No creativity! No imagination!"

Bakugo set his chopsticks down with a loud clack.

"You got beef with my kimchi hot pot, do ya?"

"Beef? No, I'm simply tossing out my thoughts," said Monoma.

"Toss some of this down your stupid throat first, then!" said Bakugo.

"I actually prepared the soup base for this hot pot," added Sato. "And Bakugo provided the spicy elements, with lots of tasting and adjusting along the way! It's not just spicy, mind you. The rich, savory blend is complex enough to complement the pork belly and veggies!"

"You poured that much love into it, Bakugo?" said Eijiro Kirishima, moved by the kimchi hot pot's stirring backstory. "That explains why it's so darn tasty!" he continued, now standing. "Listen, gang—I think we oughta accept this challenge, since there's no way our pots will lose!"

Always the types to go with the flow, Kaminari and Hanta Sero cheered on the decision, and with that, it was settled. Some brought up the concern that each taste tester might just vote for their own class's creations, but in the end, the members of classes A and B agreed to rely on the honor system; they swore on their pride as future heroes to give the prize to the tastiest hot pot of all. To start, class B would try class A's.

"Mm! Tasty!"

"I could go for ten bowls of the soy milk one!"

"Wish I could pour the kimchi broth over other food as a topping!"

"Gotta be the yosenabe, for me."

"I could seriously get addicted to the tan-tan sesame hot pot."

Class A was thrilled by the positive reactions to the food they'd made.

"You guys got good taste!" said Sato, brimming with pride.

"Hah. What'd they expect?" gloated Bakugo.

"Not bad, I guess," said Monoma, who seemed unshaken. Far from it, his smile was brimming with confidence as he reached for a pot lid.

"But the time has come for you to try our master-pieces. I now present...our first hot pot!"

Monoma removed the lid, and when the steam cleared, class A let loose a collective gasp at the sight of marbled beef, scallions, and *konjac* noodles jammed together in the bubbling broth.

"Th-that's sukiyaki!" cried Uraraka, who could barely contain the drool threatening to escape her lips.

"Sukiyaki's cheating!" roared Kirishima—a self-professed meat lover. His panic was a clear sign that he was close to breaking, and who could blame him? The salty-sweet sukiyaki stock combined with beef had a way of stimulating the primal urges of one's appetite.

"Note that we've cooked it in cast iron, no less. Impressive, isn't it?" said Monoma. "We recommend adding eggs to this one."

On cue, Honenuki, Tsuburaba, Hiryu Rin, and Niren-geki Shoda produced bowls holding raw eggs (already cracked) and began ladling the sukiyaki on top. Uraraka gulped in anticipation before downing a mouthful of sukiyaki beef and egg, which immediately made her slump over in absolute bliss.

"D-delish!" cried Kirishima, who proceeded to inhale the rest of his sample. So moved was he by the experience that onlookers half expected his clothes to rip apart and burst away in ecstasy.

"Wow," said Midoriya, preparing to switch to full-on analysis mode. "The savory beef is complemented by the sweet and salty stock! And it's so tender and buttery that my tongue practically slices clean through it! Combine that with a fresh raw egg, and you get a rich blend that I can only describe as 'happiness in flavor form.' But to be honest, the vegetables have even more potential for greatness than the meat. Boiling them in

stock with all that melted fat creates perfect harmony with their innate sweetness and freshness! And the egg is the ideal finishing touch to bring it all together. Yes…the egg is the conductor, the meat is the vocalist… and the various vegetables are the orchestra, forming a grand opera of—"

"Nobody asked for a freakin' metaphor!" said Bakugo, tossing an empty plastic bottle. The impromptu projectile wove its way between Sero, Kaminari, and Fumikage Tokoyami to bounce squarely off Midoriya's noggin.

"*Excellente* aim. ☆" Midoriya's neighbor, Yuga Aoyama, raised his wineglass of soda in Bakugo's direction.

"Heh. The tide turns toward the sukiyaki," said Monoma to himself, observing how enthralled class A was by the first offering.

"I dun think our hot pots have thrown in the towel just yet!" shot back Kirishima.

"Your tune will change when you try our second," said Monoma, lifting the lid off the other pot. It contained some sort of white fish and vegetables.

"Is that s'posed to be seafood stew?" asked Kaminari. "But I only see that one kind of fish. Kinda lacking, yeah?"

"Enough talk. Have at it," said Monoma, with the confidence of a man who'd already won. His classmates distributed bowls with a bit of the white fish topped with ponzu soy sauce, scallions, and a puree of grated radish and carrot.

"W-what the heck? Too tasty!" said Kaminari, tears forming in his eyes. It was such an emotional response that the others half expected his clothes to burst off.

"Ribbit!" said Asui.

"A delight for the senses!" said Tokoyami.

"Yum!" said Dark Shadow. All of class A's taste testers shuddered in ecstasy, overcome by the ordinary-looking white fish. All were astonished by the flavor, though none had yet identified what type of fish it was. None, that is, except for Yaoyorozu, who had been focusing on her bite for a moment.

"I believe this is…longtooth grouper," she said. No one seemed to be familiar with the species.

"A sea fish of the Perciformes order and Serranidae family," she continued. "Perches, sea bass, and groupers, if you will. Similar to the saw-edged perch found in Kyushu. In any case, they say that consuming longtooth grouper will leave one dissatisfied with all other

fishes for the rest of one's days, so impeccable is its flavor. Making this the king of all hot pots, I'm afraid."

"She's not wrong—it's a high-grade catch, that grouper," said Monoma. "Shishida's family sent us some, just for this purpose."

"M-must've been pricey, huh…" said Uraraka, nearly trembling at the thought.

"Not at all, in this case. They themselves received it as a year-end gift," said Jurota Shishida, whose beastly appearance was at odds with his elite upbringing and impeccable etiquette.

"A bank-breaking fish…as a year-end gift…" mumbled Uraraka in disbelief.

"Pull it together, Ochaco," said Asui, handing her friend a drink.

Monoma stood and addressed the room.

"We've all tasted every hot pot, yes? Now it's time to vote! Sit yourself down in front of your pick!"

The kids were reluctant to follow his orders, and Kaminari voiced what was on everyone's mind.

"They were all super tasty! It's like you're asking us to pick a favorite family member or something!"

"Too bad! In a competition, you have to choose. Now do it!" urged Monoma.

They'd staked their pride as future heroes on picking honestly, so they began to shuffle around. Most of the votes wound up concentrated around the sukiyaki and grouper stew.

"Aw, c'mon, dudes!" said a shocked Kirishima, who'd picked the kimichi pot. "Even you, Bakugo? You went for the grouper?"

Bakugo revealed his plate, on which only a small lump of the radish puree remained, topped with ample chili powder.

"It was good," he said.

"No wonder they call it the king of the hot pots. I've learned a lot, today," said Sato, wearing the profound look of a humbled top chef. He had also chosen the grouper stew. Midoriya and many others had similar expressions, having been unable to resist the flavor of the prohibitively expensive fish.

"Heh… The votes are in, and class B wins by a land-slide! Ha ha ha ha!" said Monoma, unaware that his classmates were looking almost apologetic. He was only getting started.

"And since you've lost, I believe the rules call for some kind of punishment, right?" he said, bloodlust in his eyes and voice.

"Nobody said a damn thing about that!" protested Bakugo, speaking on behalf of his own stunned classmates. Monoma was undeterred.

"Oh? I suppose you'd rather say 'Good match, friend' and have us go on our merry way? No, it's only natural for losers to suffer a penalty. Or should we assume that class A is a bunch of pacifist peaceniks?"

"I wouldn't say that," said Ida. "But these rules ought to have been made clear before the competition began!"

"Tell me, president of class A," said Monoma. "We all hope to be heroes someday, right? Do you think villains will politely lay out the rules of engagement before doing battle?"

"Do you mean to say that you and the rest of class B are playing the part of dastardly, unreasonable villains in some sort of simulation, for our benefit? How admirably self-sacrificing of you!" said Ida, fully seduced by Monoma's tactics. Before the rest of class B could say, "That was never actually the plan," or the rest of class A could stop the runaway Ida train, it was decided.

"Very well!" said Ida. "It's only sportsmanlike that we accept our penalty!"

"Speak for yourself!" screamed Bakugo, to no avail.

Monoma declared that class A would face penalty by *yaminabe*, which was a fun enough idea for Kaminari, Ashido, and Toru Hagakure to change their tune and be on board.

"What's a 'yaminabe'?" asked Todoroki.

"I've never experienced it myself," started Midoriya, "but you used to see them in old comics a lot. The *yami* means 'dark,' and *nabe* means 'pot,' so we'll have to eat from a hot pot in complete darkness, with no way of knowing what we're about to put in our mouths or what's been added to the mix. It works as a penalty since people can add ingredients that you…normally wouldn't expect, so to speak."

"I see!" said Ida, who'd also needed an explanation.

"When I first heard about the yaminabe, I thought it was *yummynabe*, like a yummy pot of food!" said Tsunotori, who, as usual, was excited to experience a new aspect of Japanese culture. Even the other members of class B, who'd seemed embarrassed by Monoma's little rampage, were starting to express interest. Many had

learned of the concept from comic books, but few had ever participated in one in real life.

And so, the yaminabe prep began.

Bakugo started to slink off to his room, saying, "Like hell you're roping me into this," but a dash of Monoma's standard provocation was all it took to rope him into it.

With the room illuminated only by the glowing fire of the tabletop gas burner, class A closed their eyes, and class B tossed various ingredients into the pot.

"Hmm? Something smells sweet!"

"That all better be *food*! Cuz I just heard something go 'clank' on the bottom."

"Now I'm smelling...something rotten? Fermented, maybe?"

Every new contribution to the pot added its own unique smell, resulting in a complex, unholy blend of aromas. Class A was growing steadily warier about their prospects, so Kendo did her best to reassure them.

"Don't worry! Everything in there is definitely edible!"

"I wouldn't be so quick to claim that," quipped Monoma, not wanting his rivals to feel reassured.

"Knock it off, Monoma," said Kendo.

"A feast of darkness..." said Tokoyami.

"A pitch-black banquet..." said Shihai Kuroiro. Both boys couldn't have felt more at home in the dark room as the pot bubbled away.

"And now, the yaminabe is served!"

Monoma's triumphant declaration echoed through the dark.

"Hold up a sec!" said Kaminari, who was fidgeting around. "I gotta use the little boys' room! Too much soda, y'know!"

"Ah, me too!" said Ojiro.

"Samesies!" said Ashido.

"*Moi* as well, ☆" said Aoyama. "But rest assured that even the toilet bowl will sparkle and twinkle when I'm through with it. ☆"

"You guys chicken, or what?" mocked Sero.

"Naw! I'll chow down as soon as I get back! Though, uh, don't wait up on our account," said Kaminari.

There had to be an exception in the rules for natural bodily functions, so the four members of class A were allowed to shuffle off (carefully, in the darkness) to the nearest bathroom.

"Tell me, class A! Are you ready to face the yaminabe?" said Monoma.

Resigned to their fate and filled with trepidation, the kids of class A began taking turns to pluck something out of the pot. The chivilrous Kirishima volunteered to go first.

"Huh? What the heck...? Kinda limp... Smells like a veggie... Tasty, though!"

"That's gotta be the spinach I tossed in! It'll power you up!" said Tetsutetsu.

"Something actually good for the ol' bod? Thanks a ton, Tetsutetsu!"

And so the bonds of friendship between Kirishima and Tetsutetsu were made even stronger by a bit of spinach in the dark. Next up was Ida, who, as class president, felt obligated to take one for the team.

"Here I go..." he said nervously, as he grabbed something with his chopsticks, popped it into his mouth, and began to chew.

"It's quite...gloopy. Mushy, perhaps? Like a lump of pure gluten..."

"That would be the body of the Lord..." said Shiozaki.

"A *body*, you say?" said a shocked Ida.

"In the Christian faith, *bread* symbolizes the body of Christ," explained Yaoyorozu.

"Me next!" said Uraraka. Her random pick made a satisfying crunch as she bit down and kept chewing. "It's cucumber!" she said.

"That's from me," said Yanagi. Uraraka chewed a bit more and offered a final thought.

"Y'know, that's not half bad!"

"I might as well go," said Asui. Her tongue analyzed the hard, round item she had plucked from the pot.

"Is this a hard candy?" she asked.

"Bingo! It's a lozenge!" said Komori, following up with her distinctive "shroom, shroom" chuckle.

"Once the broth washes off, the lozenge alone is tasty enough," said Asui, as she continued rolling the candy over her tongue. Hearing it swish around, Tsuburaba was reminded of the joint battle training exercise when Asui had wrapped up his entire body with her long frog-like tongue. He suddenly felt a kinship with the candy in her mouth.

Sero was up next, and his prize was something soft and mushy.

"Yech! Is this a piece of apple?" he said.

"Yes, it is!" said Tsunotori. "I put the apple in the pot! I love apples! In anime, people often put fruit in the yaminabe!"

Tokoyami nearly gasped upon hearing this. Little Eri was already a fellow apple lover, and now Tsunotori too?

The apple-fan trio... We shall have to chat about our love of apples at some point...

Todoroki drew something hard from the pot. Something that clacked against his teeth when he tried to bite down.

"That was quite a noise, Todoroki!" said Ida.

"I hope you didn't crack a tooth?" said a worried Midoriya.

Todoroki spit the item onto his plate and poked at it with a finger.

"Too hard to eat," he said. "Some kind of shell, I think."

"That would be my escargot!" said Monoma smugly.

"I told you, nothing inedible!" said Kendo, who, in the darkness, couldn't deliver her usual chop to the neck.

"It's perfectly edible! The insides, that is," said Monoma.

Meanwhile, Tetsutetsu was getting excited.

"Well, what's the soup taste like?" he asked no one in particular.

"Kinda hard...to pin down an exact flavor," said an unenthusiastic Sero, which only served to get Tetsutetsu more worked up.

"Can I try it? Please?" he said.

"Here," said Todoroki, extending the ladle in the direction of Tetsutetsu's voice. Mineta, Sero, and several others encouraged the class B boy, saying that any *real* man would be guzzling this stuff by the mouthful, so Tetsutetsu scooped a generous portion of the mystery stew into his bowl.

"Whoa! Smells super nasty! Makin' me lose my appetite!" he said, just before chowing down anyway. A medley of mismatched ingredients went down his gullet all at once.

"Urk!" said Tetsutetsu, fighting the urge to vomit.

"Dumbass..." said Bakugo.

"Hard to describe other than gross as heck! You gotta try some, Monoma! It's real nasty!" said Tetsutetsu.

"You don't seem to grasp the point of this *penalty* exercise, you fool," said Monoma.

But the yaminabe was so disgusting that Tetsutetsu felt obligated to share the misery with his classmates, so he went around the circle, saying, "Just a bite, yeah? Nastiest thing you've ever tried, I swear!"

Honenuki, Kojiro Bondo, and Manga Fukidashi felt too guilty refusing, so they agreed to a spoonful each. All dry heaved, and Fukidashi said, "Makes a guy wanna HORK."

"May I try it too?" asked Tsunotori, who was beyond curious by this point. "*No. Not my cup of tea,*" she declared in English, after the jarring experience triggered her to switch from Japanese to her native tongue.

"How about you, Kendo?" said Tetsutetsu.

"Fine, just a little," said Kendo, agreeing impulsively. She sipped the soup and immediately wanted to hurl.

"It's bitter and sweet and pungent and sour and spicy... Yep, totally nasty!" she said.

"The bitter part's gotta be from the coffee you added, Itsuka. And I bet my natto contribution made it pungent," said Tokage nonchalantly.

"Don't forget the fermented tofu, courtesy of Rin!" added Awase.

"And I bet it's sweet cuz of Shoda's honey," said Sen Kaibara. "Plus, the ice cream I tossed in."

Others chimed in, explaining how they'd added chocolate, cake, a hamburger, potato chips, strawberry milk, a banana, pineapple, and several other foods horribly suited for a hot stew. Hearing this list left Midoriya and the others who hadn't sampled it yet trembling with fear, especially since Tetsutetsu had already scooped out the solid ingredients, leaving them only with a concentrated dose of the sickening broth. One after the other, Midoriya, Bakugo, Tokoyami, Jiro, Koda, and Hagakure gulped it down and nearly gagged. As a penalty, the yaminabe was a roaring success.

"Phew! Really needed to go," said Ashido as she and the other three finally returned from the bathroom. They too were encouraged to drink the refined broth, but they couldn't seem to scoop any up. The lights came back on and revealed that the yaminabe pot was completely empty.

"Aw, I really wanted to try some," said Kaminari, sounding disappointed. This earned side-eye from Monoma.

"I never took you for a schemer!" he said with a nasty sneer. Kaminari realized what he was being accused of and grew indignant.

"I mean it! It's not every day you get a chance to try a yaminabe," he said.

"Huh? You're suspecting us of foul play, Monoma?" said Ashido through pouted lips and puffed-out cheeks. Ojiro and Aoyama were also visibly offended—not that Monoma would ever be rattled by the likes of class A.

"Motives aside, the fact remains that some of class A managed to evade this penalty, yes? I suppose I shouldn't expect more from this gang of reprobates."

Tension suddenly filled the air, but before Kendo could deliver a karate chop to the instigator's neck, Tetsutetsu threw an arm around Monoma's shoulders.

"Sorry, guys! He's not all bad, I swear. He just can't help the trash talk sometimes!"

"Trash talk, Tetsutetsu? Hardly," said Monoma. "I'm saying that this probably doesn't sit well with our dear friends in class A. I know that class B simply wouldn't accept it if members of our ranks were to sneakily avoid a penalty."

"Hey, listen here—" said Ojiro, but Monoma cut him off.

"Of course! You can't accept it either! You four must have been eager to face your penalty! The way I see it, the only solution is another contest!"

This announcement left both classes stunned. Monoma wanted to taste those sweet, sweet class A tears again, but after the hot pot feast, most of the others present just wanted to relax.

"Another contest?"

"Ugh, enough of all that."

The girls were fed up with Monoma's nonsense, but it wasn't Bakugo's style to walk away after losing.

"Fine—but know that we're gonna achieve total victory this time," he said.

"Ooh, good attitude!" said Monoma. "And our next arena will be…"

"Not so fast. We get to pick now," said Bakugo.

"Let's not be so hasty with further contests!" said Ida. "Besides, when will we get around to discussing our work studies, per our original intentions?"

U

"A sauna endurance battle, seriously?" said Hagakure. "What the heck is fun about getting uncomfortably hot and sweaty?"

"Don't ask me. I dunno why old men love hanging out in saunas," said Komori, tilting her head in confusion.

"Mm," said Kodai, clearly agreeing with the other girls.

Despite Ida's protests, Kirishima, Tetsutetsu, and the other "manly" boys had leaped at Bakugo's suggestion for a sauna showdown. As such, every one of the boys was now in the bathing area battling it out, while the girls had stayed behind for an after-dinner tea party. Far from a stiff affair, it had mostly consisted of them just sitting around, drinking tea brewed by Yaoyorozu, eating the snacks provided by Kendo, and chatting about this, that, and the other thing.

"I actually love the sauna whenever I'm visiting a hot spring or bathhouse. I can't stand the heat for too long, but there's just something special about sipping on iced coffee once you're out of the hot box," said Kendo, between bites of dessert.

"Way to sound like some old geezer!" teased Tokage.

"Pshh, shut up…" fired back Kendo.

"I love it too! Specially the way your body, like, tightens back up when you dive into the cold bath afterward!" said Ashido, squeezing a couch cushion into her chest to illustrate.

"Eh? I hate that feeling," said Jiro, shaking her head. "What about you, Momoyao? You a fan of saunas?" she asked.

"Yes, I used ours a lot when I lived at home," said Yaoyorozu as she prepped more tea. "It's wonderful for one's metabolism."

"You got one in your house?" asked Jiro.

"Yes. My father loves a good sauna, so he imported an authentic one plank by plank from Finland," said Yaoyorozu as if this was a perfectly common thing to do. The girls of class B weren't quite aware of the Yaoyorozu family's absurd wealth, so they went a bit wild upon hearing this.

"Did I…say something wrong?" asked a trouble Yaoyorozu. Jiro, Ashido, and Hagakure—who had all

been to the mansion—reassured their friend that she hadn't committed a faux pas.

"The one in your house—is it big?" asked Tsunotori.

"I can't speak to its relative size, but it can fit about fifty people, I suppose," said Yaoyorozu.

More oohs and ahs from the class B girls.

"That's, uh, loads bigger than the ones at our local bathhouses," said Uraraka.

"If you'd like, you could all visit and use my sauna at some point?" said Yaoyorozu shyly, realizing how excited her friends were over the notion of a home sauna.

"Wow, y'mean it?"

"Yeah! Let's do it!"

"I thought you didn't like saunas, though?"

"Yeah, but it could be fun with a bunch of friends!"

"Wonderful! My parents would be delighted," said Yaoyorozu, looking pretty thrilled herself. But then she noticed that someone in the circle was having a hard time speaking up.

"Erm, what about you, Jiro…?"

Jiro fidgeted awkwardly, unable to find the words for a moment.

"You can count me out of sauna time, but I'd love to hang out at your place again, Momoyao."

"Yes, of course!"

Yaoyorozu was the shining ideal of an unpretentious modern princess, and seeing that dazzling smile almost made Jiro reconsider her "no saunas" policy. That thought was interrupted by a news bulletin on the TV.

"*This report just in: A villain arrested for robbery has escaped from the police station and is currently at-large. We're being told that this villain's Quirk is called 'Snowfall.'*"

"Uh, that police station's in the next town over. Should we be worried?" asked Uraraka.

"I'm sure they've already got heroes on the job," said Asui.

"Yeah, I bet you're right," said Uraraka with a relieved smile. Ashido took the news differently.

"Hey, you think that Snowfall Quirk could make it snow around here?" she said, shooting excited glances at the others.

"Come to think of it, it hasn't snowed this year yet, right?" said Komori. "I wouldn't mind some snow, shroom."

"We're talking about an *escaped villain* here," said Kendo with a weak smile, chiding the more eager girls.

"Sorrry!" said Ashido.

"Just saying, shroom," said Komori.

Suddenly, the girls heard a distant cry of "Hot, hot, hot!" from the boys' bathing area. They grew silent, then exchanged weary glances.

"The boys really do seem to relish these competitions," said Yaoyorozu, shaking her head with her hands on her cheeks.

"Futile conflict can only breed calamity," said Shiozaki. But Hagakure didn't quite agree, and she was hit with a flash of inspiration.

"Hey! How about we have a little contest? Like, a more peaceful one!" she said.

"Peaceful?" questioned Shiozaki. "A contest the Lord would condone?"

"Yes, sure, whatever!" said Hagakure. "How about, like, the Yamanote Line game, but instead of naming train stops, we go back and forth saying what we like about our homeroom teachers! First side to run out of things to say loses!"

The other girls were shocked by the suggestion, but they didn't hate it.

"Should we?" asked Kendo. To which they all responded, "Yeah!"

"S'gonna be pretty hard for us to lose, since there's a lot to love about our Vlad King Sensei," said Tokage, throwing down the gauntlet.

"Yeah, well, Aizawa Sensei has plenty that makes him a winner in our book," said Ashido, not backing down in the slightest. Though this game was admittedly less dramatic than the boys and their sauna, neither side here would be going down without a proper fight.

UA

Meanwhile, the boys—with towels wrapped around waists and heads—were all still in the steamy, sweltering bathing area. They'd created a makeshift sauna by placing Todoroki in the center of the room and having him fire up the heat-based side of his Quirk. The participants formed a circle around the impromptu heat source, sitting on either stools or the edge of the

bath itself. First class to throw in the proverbial towel would lose, and the temperature in the bathing area had already reached unreasonable levels.

"I have to say, Bakugo," said Monoma, with sweat dripping down his once fair but now red skin, "I'm almost impressed at how low-down and dirty you are."

"Huh?" said Bakugo.

"Isn't it true that your Quirk grows stronger the more you sweat? In other words, your body is built to withstand the heat. In my humble opinion, it takes a certain type of loser to propose a contest where he has the clear advantage."

"Hah. From where I'm standing, that sounds like a pathetic excuse for why you're about to lose," said Bakugo, who barely seemed fazed by the heat. Monoma might have been at a physical disadvantage, but he still had his sharp tongue.

"Enjoy that confidence while you can...because we still have our secret weapon to deploy! None other than Tetsutetsu!" said Monoma.

When transformed by his "Steel" Quirk, Tetsutetsu's body was capable of withstanding even Todoroki's blazing heat, but at Monoma's suggestion, he had started off the contest with his flesh and blood body.

"That's right! Still feelin' lukewarm in here, if you ask me!" he said haughtily.

"Good going, Tetsutetsu! I'm just warming up too!" said Kirishima, another confident participant with a Quirk made to withstand heat. Aoyama, however, was feeling like a steamed lobster.

"I cry *oncle*... ☆" he said before leaping into the main bath, which was filled with cold water.

Mineta also left the battlefield soon after, grumbling, "How'd I wind up surrounded by naked dudes anyway...?"

"Twinkly? Balls-for-Brains? You gotta be kidding me!" shouted Bakugo. But Mineta ignored the jab and beckoned Kaminari from within the soothingly cool water.

"Kaminari... Get over here, man. You're no fan of the heat, right?"

"Naw, I'm still...in this game!" said Kaminari, addressing Monoma more than Mineta. Sweat dripped down his face and body, but since Monoma had accused him of chickening out of the yaminabe challenge, he was determined to outlast the class B provocateur. Monoma

noticed Kaminari staring right at him and responded with a sneer. Unfortunately for him, two of his own classmates were about to wipe the smirk off his face.

"Sorry, can't take it anymore... Feels like I'm leaking all over," said Bondo.

"I'm at my limit too," said Shoda. Both boys left the Todoroki circle and stepped into the cool bath.

"Bondo! Nirengeki! You two doing okay?" said Monoma, who was capable of genuine kindness and concern when it came to his own cohort.

"Aoyama, Mineta, Bondo, Shoda—I've prepared sports drinks for just this reason. Please replenish your fluids!"

Ida scurried over to the bath from the corner of the room and grabbed a few chilled plastic bottles from the cooler he was toting. He'd been opposed to the sauna battle from the start, but if it had to happen, he would prioritize the health and safety of all involved.

"That's our Ida for ya!" said Mineta. This compliment and the words of thanks from the others made Ida feel proud.

"Only doing my duty as the president of class A!"

"We're all grateful for that, Ida," said Shoda.

"Nonsense, Shoda! You just take it easy now," said Ida.

In the middle of the oppressively sweltering sauna, here was an oasis of congeniality; class A's by-the-book president got along well with class B's sincere and honest straight shooter.

But Ida's icy cold sports drinks proved to be a curse in disguise. As the quitters gulped down sip after sip to quench their thirst, the sauna battlers less adapted to beating the heat saw only irresistible temptation.

"I can't take any more…"

"S-same here…"

"Dammit, Four-Eyes! You're screwing us over with that crap!" said Bakugo, noticing more of his classmates getting ready to quit. "Half 'n' Half! Kick the temp up a notch!"

"You sure? Okay," said Todoroki, obeying. The room suddenly got even hotter, and shrieks of "Nooo!" and "Cut it out!" rose from the boys who'd already been barely hanging on. Kaminari groaned and Monoma winced in pain, but the latter's antagonism toward class A pulled him back from the brink and drove him to give his own order to Fukidashi.

"Fukidashi! Give us an onomatopoeia that'll raise the heat!" said Monoma.

"Huh?" said Fukidashi. "Sure thing. Let's see… BLAZE BLAZE!"

Fukidashi's "Comic" Quirk allowed him to make sound effects come to life, so when he uttered "BLAZE BLAZE," a physical manifestation of the fiery words emerged and became a new heat source.

"Tch. So that's how it's gonna be?" said Bakugo. "Hey, Arms! Spin these towels around!"

He ripped the towels from the heads of the remaining participants and handed them to Shoji.

"Like this?" asked Shoji, as he used his multiple arms to swing the towels around, creating a mini cyclone of infernally hot air. This third spike in temperature brought about more moaning and groaning.

"I ain't beat yet!" said Tetsutetsu.

"Don't count me out!" said Kirishima. Neither hot-blooded boy was feeling discouraged just yet.

"Nope, I'm out…" said Midoriya, who got up and started making for the cool bath.

"Dammit, Deku! Show some guts!" screamed Bakugo, who threw a nearby bath pail so hard that it ricocheted off the floor and nailed Midoriya square in his privates.

"Urk!" grunted Midoriya, but before he could pass out and collapse, Ida rushed over and caught his friend.

"Look what you've done to Midoriya's scrotum! Oh dear... We'll have to ice the affected area!"

"Here. For Midoriya's scrotum," said Todoroki, who created a piece of ice in his right hand and slid it across the scorching floor to Ida, all while maintaining the heat from his left side.

"Much appreciated!" said Ida. He wrapped Todoroki's ice chunk in a towel and applied it to the site of the damage.

"Oww..." whimpered Midoriya, sounding like a sad puppy. Despite their focus on enduring the brutal heat, the other boys knew that pain all too well and couldn't help but sympathize.

"Another member of class A bites the dust, it seems," said Monoma.

"Huh? Deku never made it to the bath, so he's still in the game," said Bakugo.

As the two de facto leaders argued, the room kept getting hotter, until all but the most stalwart couldn't take it any longer.

"Ugh... I'm done... Let's bow out, Kaminari," whispered a pained Sero.

Kaminari had long since passed his limit in a stubborn show of defiance against Monoma, but he could tell that Monoma was just as stubborn, which only bolstered his determination. At some point, though, the heat started to rob Kaminari of his conscious mind, until he forgot what he was fighting for to begin with. His heart wavered, imagining how delicious it would feel to submerge his broiled body in the cool water of the bath.

"Hnngh..." he groaned, prepared to admit defeat at last, but in that moment, Kaminari heard a sharp, crackling sound. The temperature in the room took a nosedive, and he noticed that Todoroki was slumped over and was now producing not fire and heat, but freezing ice instead. The boys who'd been ready to call it quits—including Kaminari—rejoiced and breathed sighs of relief, but Bakugo's eyebrows tilted at deadly angles.

"What's with the cold shoulder, Half 'n' Half?"

"Why, Todoroki… Have we at last discovered *your* limit, even?" said Monoma, who, despite his own immense relief, was never one to forgo the chance to deliver a pithy comment.

"That's the ticket, Todoroki! Keep the ice coming!" said Sero.

"We wouldn't mind an ice bath right about now!" added Kaibara.

Todoroki seemed to obey, because the room kept getting cooler. The boys' broiled bodies were soothed by the below-freezing temperature, and it didn't take them long to adjust. However…

"That's too much, Todoroki!" shouted Ojiro.

"Todoroki! I believe Midoriya's scrotum is quite chilled enough!" added Ida. The boys felt like they'd been air-dropped into the Antarctic with nothing but a towel around their waists, and the cold wasn't letting up.

"All right, you… Enough of this crap!" said Bakugo, but as he attempted to stand, he muttered, "W-what's wrong with me…?" and slumped onto the floor in a heap.

"Bakugo!" shouted Kirishima, but when he tried to run to his friend, he also collapsed.

"Bakugo? Kirishima?" shouted Kaminari, who dashed over to the fallen boys. Both were fast asleep, as if they'd been knocked out.

"They're snoozing? Weird time for a power nap... Hey, Todoroki, quit it with the cold stuff... Wait. Todoroki too?" said Kaminari, realizing that the source of the cold was also asleep.

"Hey, Midoriya! Ida? Koda?" said Ojiro, checking three of his classmates.

"Tokoyami? Shoji, Sero, and Sato too? What could be the matter?" said Aoyama.

Over in the cool bath, Shoda was frantically trying to keep Mineta's and Bondo's heads above water.

"Tetsutetsu? Honenuki?" said Monoma, noticing that his own classmates had slumped over.

"Whoa, Bondo and Fukidashi too?" said Kaibara

"What the heck is going on here...?" muttered Kaminari, now frozen to the bone as he surveyed the bizarre scene.

UA

Meanwhile, the girls in the common area were dealing with similar problems. In the middle of their good-natured battle over which class had the better homeroom teacher, Uraraka, Asui, Yaoyorozu, Jiro, Hagakure, and Kendo had suddenly fallen into sleeplike trances—and what's more, some of their Quirks were misfiring. Uraraka was floating across the room, Asui was hopping around and croaking like a real frog, Yaoyorozu was producing matryoshka dolls nonstop, and Jiro just lay there, not moving a muscle.

"What's the deal, girls? Cut that out!" said Ashido, the only remaining class A girl with her wits about her. She ran around shaking her friends like rag dolls, but they refused to snap out of it.

"Itsuka? What's wrong, Itsuka?" said Tokage.

"Pony won't wake up either," said Yanagi, sounding worried. Like Jiro, Kendo and Tsunotori had fallen into a heavy, motionless sleep.

"Get down here, Uraraka! That's dangerous, Asui!" shouted Ashido. Uraraka had floated all the way up to

the high ceiling and now seemed to be stuck, while Asui was clinging to the glass of the common area's tall windows.

"Mm!" said Kodai, eying the army of matryoshkas Yaoyorozu was unwittingly creating. In truth, Kodai didn't hate the idea of a room full of nesting dolls.

ᕡ

Back in the boys' bathing area, a few of the sudden sleepers were also firing off their Quirks.

"Hot, hot! Wait, that's cold! Ack, hot again!"

Thanks to Todoroki's "Half-Cold Half-Hot" Quirk, the room was violently fluctuating between murderously hot sauna and frozen meat locker. Sero's "Tape" was also haphazardly launching from his elbows, plastering Ojiro, Aoyama, Kaibara, and Fukidashi to the floor and walls.

"Ugh, not my tail!" said Ojiro, knowing how painful it would be to rip the tape from his fluffy tail tip.

"Hot? Cold? Please, do make up your mind, ☆" said a weary Aoyama.

"I've had enough!" said a pissed-off Kaibara as he started to tear away the tape.

"Hang on!" said Tsuburaba, who'd managed to escape the tape storm. "Lemme set up an Air Prison for us, and…"

But before he could use his "Solid Air" Quirk to protect the remaining boys from the heat, cold, and tape, the floor suddenly turned soft and began to undulate. Honenuki's "Softening" Quirk was to blame, since his limp hand had touched the floor as he fell asleep. Meanwhile, Ida's engine-powered legs were pumping through thin air as he lay on his side, Bondo was squirting glue everywhere, and Mineta's "Pop Off" balls were scattered about.

"What on earth is this about?" shouted Monoma, surveying the chaos.

"Dunno, but we gotta help everyone!" said Kaminari.

"Right, of course," said Monoma, suddenly sounding like he'd come to grips. "First, we need to get everyone away from Todoroki."

Monoma's quick thinking was just the thing to spur the others to action. Tsuburaba's Solid Air provided them with footholds and shields to protect themselves

from Mineta's balls and Bondo's glue, and Togaru Kamakiri's "Razor Sharp" Quirk helped cut through Sero's tape. Before long, they'd managed to drag their sleeping friends out of the bathing area. Only Todoroki remained inside, since it seemed like the best place to contain him while his Quirk continued to misfire. As for the boys who were flailing around in their trances, Monoma used Sero's tape (which he copied with his own "Copy" Quirk) to bind them and keep them from hurting themselves. Similarly, the girls had used Shiozaki's vines to grab Uraraka and Asui off the ceiling and window, and for the time being, they'd wrapped the pair in heavy blankets, for safety's sake.

Reunited, the still-lucid boys and girls agreed that they'd better contact their teachers for help, but when they moved toward the front entrance, they were stunned by what they saw outside: snow was piled up on the other side of the window, to a degree one might expect in the frigid northern regions. The kids then tried calling the teachers but couldn't get through. Perhaps they were busy dealing with the sudden snowfall?

"Where'd all this snow come from?"

"Ah, I think I might know..." said Ashido, who went on to explain to the boys that an escaped villain's Quirk might be behind this. Even the girls—who'd heard the news story firsthand—hadn't noticed the snow until now.

"So, we can't reach our teachers, and it's likely that this snow has them sealed in as well. Which means we somehow have to deal with this crisis ourselves," said Monoma.

"Somehow? How, exactly? We dunno what's causing this, even..."

"I think the hot pot might be to blame," said Monoma, sounding uncharacteristically earnest. The others gasped, and Monoma continued.

"Note that only those who sampled the yaminabe have been affected," he said.

"Right... That'd explain why Ojiro, Aoyama, Ashido, and I are okay," said Kaminari, remembering their trip to the bathroom. But Shishida wasn't convinced.

"If so, why are some of our schoolmates merely sleeping, while others are firing off their Quirks?" he asked.

"Maybe it's about the amount they ate?" suggested Tsuburaba. "Tetsutetsu was gorging himself on the stuff."

"But what was wrong with the yaminabe? We all agreed only to add edible stuff," said Yanagi.

"Yeah, I just tossed in some strawberry milk," said Tsuburaba.

"I picked squid ink," said Kuroiro.

"And I added some nastycap mushrooms I found in the forest, shroom," said Komori. The other members of class B volunteered their own contributions, until only Monoma remained.

"I put in escargot...*salmiak* licorice...*schnecken* gummies, and..."

"You added more than one thing? And salmiak and those schnecken things are famous for being the nastiest candies around!" said Kaminari angrily. Incidentally, Aizawa was a big fan of salmiak licorice.

"There was no rule stating only one item per person. Anyhow...my fourth thing was some more of those nastycaps that Komori must have forgotten," said Monoma, as if it were an afterthought.

"Huh? I totally added all the nastycaps I brought..." said Komori. After a second, she gasped.

"Wait. Don't tell me it was the ones in that plastic bag?"

"Yes? I assumed you were trying to spare class A from too much nastiness," said Monoma.

"Those weren't nastycaps! They were quirksnoozes! Poison mushrooms!" said Komori.

"Huh?"

"If any quirksnoozes were in that broth, then just a sip would be enough to put someone in a coma! Eating an actual piece of one makes your Quirk go wild! When I spotted some growing out there, I made sure to pick them all so I could dispose of them properly later!"

As it dawned on everyone that Monoma was unwittingly responsible for poisoning their classmates, they turned to the guilty party and gave him a death stare. He might've attempted to make an excuse, but the anger in their eyes caused him to reconsider.

"Sorry..." said Monoma.

The simple apology felt incredibly admirable coming from him, so the others decided not to pile on the guilt further. Besides, saving their sleeping friends was the top priority now.

"So, how do we counteract the quirksnooze poison?" asked Kaminari.

"There's only one way, shroom..." said Komori. "We gotta feed them dequirksnooze!"

Kaminari was puzzled.

"The quirksnooze? Isn't that what started this problem?"

"Not *the* quirksnooze. Dequirksnooze! It's another type of mushroom that grows near quirksnooze shrooms."

"Did you happen to pick some of those too?" asked Kaminari.

"Nah. Those ones aren't poisonous, but they don't taste good either, shroom," said Komori.

"I guess that means someone's gotta go mushroom picking..." said Kaminari. This prompted the others to glance toward the window, but the snow had already piled up too high for them to see even a sliver of the outside world.

"I'll do it."

"Seriously, Monoma...?" said Kaminari.

"This seems to be my fault, so it's only right," said Monoma matter-of-factly. "Komori—can you give me detailed directions to the spot?"

Kaminari scowled. He knew it would be an uphill challenge if Monoma went it alone.

"Guess I gotta come with you!" said Kaminari.

"You?" said a shocked Monoma. "But you're useless."

"Huh?"

Kaminari only had good intentions, so the casual insult stung.

"It'd be dangerous out there all alone!" he said, getting up in Monoma's face. "And I can be useful! Like, as a battery!"

"Hmph. I guess I can't stop you from tagging along."

"Knock it off, man. That whole hot-and-cold shtick isn't cute at all when you do it!"

Kaminari was really getting worked up now, and the others were concerned.

"No need to get bent out of shape, Kaminari," said Ojiro.

"Yeah! You know how this guy is," said Kaibara, not exactly defending Monoma.

The group talked it over a bit more and decided that the dequirksnooze expedition team would consist of Monoma, Kaminari, Ojiro, Aoyama, Kaibara, and Komori.

Everyone else would keep watch over their comatose friends, in case of any additional Quirk outbursts.

Komori was a key member of the team—since she was the one who knew the mushrooms' location—so naturally, Kuroiro also volunteered. The others told him to stay behind, however, since his ability to meld with black objects wasn't suited to venturing out into a fresh, white snowscape.

At first they assumed they could trek about on top of the snow, but then they realized it had already reached as high as the third floor of the building. Falling through the top and getting buried could be deadly, so the team decided to tunnel through on the ground instead. Before setting out, they changed into heavy clothes and coats, and Monoma copied some of the more useful Quirks available, even if he could only keep them in reserve for about five minutes.

When the front door refused to open more than an inch or two, Monoma reached through the crack and used Honenuki's Softening Quirk to make the snow on the other side a little more cooperative. Once past the doorway, Kaibara took charge.

"My turn now!" he said. He spinning arms acted like drills that could carve a tunnel through the snow, all while referencing GPS to keep them on track.

Maybe Monoma was right... I am kinda useless out here.

Seeing the others contribute suddenly made Kaminari disappointed in himself, especially after all his big talk earlier.

"What's wrong?" asked Ojiro, who'd noticed that Kaminari was in a funk.

"Nah, nothing," said Kaminari, turning to Ojiro with a smile. But then he glanced ahead at Monoma, who was near the head of the pack. It had mostly been Monoma who'd put together the mushroom-hunting plan, and Kaminari was dumbfounded that the class B provocateur had gone about it with such a level head, given his usual propensity for snark and sarcasm.

He can really get it done, huh...

Kaminari scowled at his own realization before trying to get into a different headspace. The sooner they pulled off this operation, the sooner all his friends would be safe and sound again. Even if it meant being the group's whipping boy. But just as Kaminari was

getting his groove back, Monoma said, "Kaibara! Stop for a second!"

"Why, what's up?"

"I just lost the GPS signal. Most likely because of the snow."

"What now, shroom?" said Komori.

Monoma thought for a moment.

"We know the general direction, so keep heading that way. We should run into a main road soon. After that, we turn left, and we should hit the forest before long."

Kaibara started drilling again, but they never reached the promised road. They needed to get their bearings, so they began tunneling up to the surface of the snow, and the nimble Ojiro created footholds before hauling the others up with him.

Up top, a full-blown blizzard was raging. Monoma used an air shield courtesy of Tsuburaba's Quirk to guard his face from the wind and snow in order to get a better look around them. Sadly, his flashlight was rendered all but useless by the blizzard.

"I believe it is my time to shine, ☆" said Aoyama, who spun around and fired off his "Navel Laser" to illuminate their surroundings.

"Ah! Over there!" shouted Komori, pointing at one particular tree in the forest.

"Sorry I got so off course!" said Kaibara.

"We're all just doing our best in this emergency," said Monoma. "But how about your arms? Not feeling frostbitten yet, I hope?"

"They still got some spin in 'em. Hurting a little, though."

Monoma inspected Kaibara's arms—which had just plowed through tons of snow—and said, "Let's take a break."

"B-but I can still..." protested Kaibara.

"No. The cold will shut down your body before you know it, so taking a bit of time to warm back up is the most efficient option. Besides, it'll only slow us down if you're a shivering mess," said Monoma.

Kaminari realized his own hands were shivering too. The heat near the ground was preserved to some extent by the thick layer of snow on top, but the cold was still gnawing away at their bodies. And above the snow? The windchill from the brutal blizzard made it feel like minus twenty degrees Celsius. Komori was curled into a ball and clinging to Ojiro's tail for dear life, and Aoyama

was shivering violently while covering his stomach with his hands.

Luckily, Monoma had copied Todoroki's Quirk, but he found it tricky to restrict the fire and heat to just his fingertips; it spread up his arm until his sleeve caught on fire.

"Careful!" said Kaminari, who grabbed a lump of snow with his shivering hands and pressed it against Monoma's arm, putting out the fire.

"It-it's out, right? Yeah. Good. You're not burned?" said Kaminari, with clear concern in his voice. Monoma was caught off guard for a moment, but it didn't take long for the sneer to return to his lip.

"Maybe you're not useless after all," he said.

"Dammit, Monoma…" said Kaminari, but his anger over the backhanded compliment subsided when he noticed a hint of embarrassment in Monoma's expression. Maybe the snark was only skin-deep? That realization was good enough for Kaminari.

Monoma gave Todoroki's Quirk another go, and the team huddled around the makeshift campfire, using Tsuburaba's air shields to construct an invisible tent.

"Never has warmth felt so lovely, ☆" said Aoyama, stating what was on all their minds.

"Now, we're nearly there," said Monoma, looking as serious as ever. "It's up to us to save the others. Class B is counting on us. Might as well help class A too, while we're at it."

"While we're at it, huh?" said Kaminari.

"Hard for you to sound cool with snot dripping down your face," quipped Kaibara, prompting Monoma to sniffle loudly as he stood back up.

"All right, let's go!"

"Yeah!"

They trudged through the blizzard toward the forest—on top of the snow this time—calling out to each other as they went so as not to lose anyone. Once they reached the tree line, more bursts of Aoyama's laser helped Komori spot the tree in question.

"That's the one, shroom!" she cried.

"Great! Leave this to me!" said Kaibara. He drilled down to the base of the tree but stopped when he got close, for fear of damaging the precious mushrooms. The others started shoving aside the snow that covered the

roots of the tree until Kaminari felt something squishy against his gloved fingertips.

"I think I found it!" he said.

"Yup!" confirmed Komori. She brushed away the snow surrounding the dequirksnooze mushroom and at last claimed the prize. The team cheered, with high fives all around, but Monoma didn't allow them to rest on their laurels.

"The job's not done. We need to get this back to the others," he said.

"Darn right! No time to lose," said Kaminari.

"But first, I need you all to promise me something," said Monoma.

"What's that?"

"Not a word about any of this to Vlad King Sensei."

"Huh?"

"I only barely passed last term's final exams," explained Monoma. "If he finds out I'm responsible for this mess, I'll be stuck taking remedial lessons, which means no work study for me!"

Kaminari and the others were agape, unsure how to respond to Monoma's deadly sincere request. Basically, he didn't want to get in trouble for screwing up.

"Are you for real, Monoma?" said Kaibara.

"What's your own problem got to do with this one, shroom?" said Komori. Monoma's classmates weren't having it, so he had to go on the offensive.

"I know you wouldn't want to cause Vlad Sensei any grief!"

"Which wouldn't be an issue if you hadn't almost failed your tests!" said Kaibara.

"Maybe it just so happens that that's all I'm capable of!" spat Monoma.

Kaminari suddenly recalled how Monoma was the only member of class B sentenced to remedial lessons during their forest training camp. He was a quick-witted strategist in battle, but apparently academics were not his forte.

"Naw, I get it!" said Kaminari, with a glint of understanding in his eyes. He was painfully aware of how it felt to struggle with written tests. At first, Monoma didn't know how to feel about the schmaltzy camaraderie Kaminari was pushing, but then he realized he'd found a willing accomplice, so he grinned.

"You'll keep your mouth shut, then?" asked Monoma.

"You bet. And I'll tell everyone who got poisoned to keep mum too!" said Kaminari.

"No, don't tell them anything at all! They don't need to know either!" said Monoma.

Class B comrades or not, the indignant Kaibara and Komori had been prepared to spill the beans to their teacher, but seeing Monoma and Kaminari quibble made them—as well as Ojiro and Aoyama—burst out laughing. They all understood Monoma's desire for a work study, so in the end, they agreed to keep quiet.

The blizzard had died down in the meantime, so the trip back to the dorm building was much easier than the initial trek. As the conquering heroes chopped up the hard-won mushroom and fed it to their afflicted friends, they told the others who'd been holding the fort not to inform the victims or teachers about the accidental poisoning. One by one, their classmates came out of the deep sleep.

"What the hell hit me..." said Bakugo groggily.

"Seems like a case of hot pot gone bad," said Kaminari, while shooting Monoma a knowing glance. Monoma flashed a sly grin underneath his feigned clueless expression.

"The hot pot?" said Bakugo.

"What, did someone add something rotten?" asked Hagakure.

The poisoning victims weren't completely satisfied with the hand-waving explanation about the hot pot, but Monoma knew just how to convince them.

"That's how it is with yaminabe," he said. "You can never be sure what's going into the mix."

"That's rich coming from the guy who suggested it!" said Kaibara, unable to hold back.

Needless to say, classes A and B swore off hot pots for a while.

The tumultuous first night of the term was winding down, and tomorrow the students would be busy with classes and work studies. Perhaps they wouldn't have been quite so excited for spring if only they'd known of the horrors that fast approached.

A Note from the Creator

Since the arc I've been working on lately in the main manga series is quite frankly way too serious in tone, getting more of these slice-of-life scenes is an absolute joy! Thank you as always, Yoshi Sensei!

KOHEI HORIKOSHI

A Note from the Author

Celebration! Volume 5!
MHA makes my heart race with both
excitement and anxiety. It's working
overtime. Still, happy days.

ANRI YOSHI

MY HERO ACADEMIA:
SCHOOL BRIEFS—UNDERGROUND DUNGEON

Written by Anri Yoshi
Original story by Kohei Horikoshi
Cover and interior design by Shawn Carrico
Translation by Caleb Cook

BOKU NO HERO ACADEMIA YUUEI HAKUSHO © 2016 by Kohei Horikoshi, Anri Yoshi
All rights reserved.
First published in Japan in 2016 by SHUEISHA Inc., Tokyo.
English translation rights arranged by SHUEISHA Inc.

Published by VIZ Media, LLC
P.O. Box 77010
San Francisco, CA 94107

Library of Congress Cataloging-in-Publication Data

Names: Horikoshi, Kōhei, 1986- author, artist. | Yoshi, Anri, author. |
  Cook, Caleb D., translator.
Title: Underground dungeon / original concept by Kohei Horikoshi ; novel by
  Anri Yoshi ; translation by Caleb Cook
Description: San Francisco : VIZ Media, 2021. | Series: My hero academia:
  school briefs ; vol. 5 | Summary: The students of class 1-A are getting
  ready for the end-of-the-year holidays but they get a big surprise when
  their big winter cleaning leads to a crazy discovery.
Identifiers: LCCN 2021021115 (print) | LCCN 2021021116 (ebook) | ISBN
  9781974724079 (paperback) | ISBN 9781974728435 (ebook)
Subjects: CYAC: Heroes--Fiction. | High schools--Fiction. |
  Schools--Fiction. | Ability--Fiction. | Fantasy.
Classification: LCC PZ7.1.H6636 Un 2021 (print) | LCC PZ7.1.H6636 (ebook)
  | DDC [Fic]--dc23
LC record available at https://lccn.loc.gov/2021021115
LC ebook record available at https://lccn.loc.gov/2021021116

Printed in the U.S.A.

10 9 8 7 6 5 4 3 2 1
First printing, October 2021

viz.com

Adventure on the high seas continue in these stories featuring the characters of **One Piece**!

NOVEL

ONE PIECE

Ace's Story

Complete in two volumes!

CREATED BY
Eiichiro Oda

WRITTEN BY
Sho Hinata (Book 1)
Tatsuya Hamazaki (Book

Get the backstory on Luffy's brother Ace! These two volumes contain the origin story of Luffy's adopted brother Ace, and tales of his thrilling quest fo the legendary One Piece treasure.

VIZ

The best-selling paranormal action adventure manga series
Bleach **continues in novel form as an all-new threat arises!**

Can't Fear Your Own World

Original Story by
Tite Kubo

Written by
Ryohgo Narita

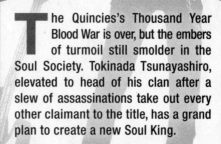

The Quincies's Thousand Year Blood War is over, but the embers of turmoil still smolder in the Soul Society. Tokinada Tsunayashiro, elevated to head of his clan after a slew of assassinations take out every other claimant to the title, has a grand plan to create a new Soul King.

Complete in Three Volumes!

VIZ